DRACULA
BEYOND STOKER

Issue 8

DBS Press

Dracula Beyond Stoker
Issue 8

Tucker Christine
editor

Edward G. Pettit
Shannon Vare Christine
consulting editors

Published by DBS Press
ISBN - 978-1-963391-14-5 (Paperback)
ISBN - 978-1-963391-15-2 (e-book)
May, 2026

www.dbspress.com
www.draculabeyondstoker.com

Contents

Letter From the Editor — 5

To End This Monstrous Cycle — 7
by Emily Elledge

Tomb of the Widergänger — 17
by Jonathan Maberry

Papers More — 33
by Brandon Keaton

A Long Night in Wisburg — 51
by Caolán Mac an Aircinn

Abraham Versus the Abhartach — 63
by Ryan Charles Lieb

Voileta's Life of Grim Purpose — 79
by David Rider

Ever Blooming — 99
by Noemi Novembre

Van Helsing's Guests — 107
by Kay Hanifen

A Change of Perspective — 123
by Bill Cozza

Smoke and Mirrors — 139
by Mark Oxbrow

Strange Bedfellows — 163
by Henry Herz

Van Helsing Syndrome — 181
by Connor Boyle

Poison in the Darkness — 191
by Rita Oakes

The Darkest Obsession — 217
by Maxwell I. Gold

30 April

My dearest reader,—

If Mina Harker is the heart and soul of *Dracula*, then Abraham Van Helsing is its mind—its rational, yet open mind. A man of science, of letters, and of law, the word "vampire" should never pass his lips, but Van Helsing knows there are things that lurk beyond reason.

In this issue, we follow the professor across a range of adventures, both before the novel and after. Here, he is more than a guide or mentor—he is the one who confronts the darkness directly.

Doctor. Teacher. Scientist. Lawyer. Each role becomes a tool in his fight against vampires, monsters, and loss. He does not waver. He does not cower. He does not give up. He asks only that you believe…believe in things that you cannot.

As ever,

TUCKER

To End This Monstrous Cycle

By Emily Elledge

On The Bullebak

*(From the notes of Dr. Abraham Van Helsing
after a field study in Utrecht, 1861)*

The Bullebak, ranging in size from 180-250cm, has a scaled exterior observed in a variety of blue and green colors, with an ability to spend large periods of time either under or above water, making this creature semi-aquatic. It has long, dagger-like teeth and thick claws suitable for hunting or scavenging, similar to those of other omnivorous, semi-aquatic animals, and these claws are deftly used for digging in the sand, either to create sound structures or to search for crustaceans. Happy to swim in the open sea, freshwater lakes, and the Amstel River, as well as the brackish canals of Amsterdam, the Bullebak has large, glowing eyes, likely the result of some form of naturally or supernaturally occurring luminescence. The Bullebak has the ability to shape-shift, manipulate water with its mind, and to communicate across vast distances, though only children and animals seem to be able to hear its call. It is a solitary creature, only engaging with its kind to mate before promptly parting ways, much like the less inconspicuous Platypus. Bullebak have been rumored to have a history of luring children to the water's edge for the purpose of drowning them, but such events are exceedingly rare, and reasons for this behavior have yet to be ascertained.

Netherlands, 1864

Bodies, at least ten of them, were strewn about Scheveningen beach, their flesh stripped, chest cavities cracked open like walnuts. Their blood wetted the sand in morbidly scarlet tide pools. The sea was slate and cold as corpses, laughing along the shore to spite the splay of viscera.

A pale man with a broad nose and reddish curls poking out from beneath a black, wide-brimmed hat, swatted at circling crabs as he surveyed the dead. He was visiting his ailing mother when he was called out to investigate the beach.

"Well, Doctor?" asked a foreign fisherman with a throaty French accent and a face marbled with liver spots.

"These men were maimed. Rather nonsensically, it seems," replied the Doctor. "Fishermen, merchants, conducting business at the docks were killed by something...inhuman. But this was not the work of some mindless, hungry animal. No...all their parts appear to be accounted for."

The Doctor took a piece of driftwood and used it to guide a coil of intestines back into one man's flayed abdomen, whose white beard was peppered with drops of blood, his mouth purple, gaping. His body made a terrible squelching sound when reunited with its innards.

"Call for the coroner," said the Doctor, stooping to gather sutures from his bag, beside a small bundle of pink tulips. "I will help him collect the victims. And then I must begin searching for what did this."

The Doctor already knew what creature was responsible for the murders, though he wouldn't dare say; he had a flare for mystery, and for theatrics—and all this besides, he knew the faces of these men. But when last he saw them, their features were youthful, their limbs strong and intact. He had first encountered them, and their killer, when he was very small, on a day similarly bright and beguiling.

Netherlands, 1836

A small boy, no more than seven years of age, bounced along beside his mother, holding onto her skirts with one hand, and fidgeting in the pocket of his woolen breeches with the other. He had a shock of tangled red hair that flopped in front of his pale blue eyes. His mother, with her deep complexion and dark hair, could be wholly unrelated to him, were it not for their shared feature of a sideways slant of the mouth, which seemed twisted into a perpetual, good humored smirk. On that day, however, her mouth was turned down at both corners, for the general flow of the crowd was agonizingly slow. People kept stopping in the middle of the cobbled street, passing whispers to one another and circulating rumpled fliers among themselves. When mother and child finally reached their destined flower stand, she spoke in a low, clipped voice to the vendor.

"Good morning, Hendrik," she said.

The vendor grunted, "Aleida."

"What has everyone buzzing about today?" She asked through her teeth, eyeing the multi-hued tulips wrapped in soft brown paper.

Hendrik snatched a flier from the hands of a passerby. The stranger looked as if he might start shouting, but, taking in Hendrik's wide, bloodshot eyes and calloused fist, he must have thought better of it and only skulked away.

Aleida read the flier, her little boy pulling on her arm to take a peek. It read:

Nixie or Bullebak? Beware the water!

It had a messy, poorly hatched illustration of a creature with dripping teeth and bulging eyes. The font was hastily printed, some of the letters smearing away.

"So, everyone's going on about fairytales?" Aleida scoffed.

"Four bodies were found washed up on the beach yesterday," said Hendrik, "*Children.* There's been talk about sightings of a strange beast lurking about the water, whether Nixie or Bullebak, who can be sure? Best stay away from the beach and not chance it anyway, I say. My own mother warned me of the Bullebak," Hendrik shuddered.

"Nonsense," said Aleida, balling up the flier, but her fingers worrying at the cross around her neck betrayed her superstition.

"Run along and play, now, Abraham, and meet me back at the train station in an hour. Don't be late. The pink ones, please, Hendrik."

"Special occasion?" asked Hendrik, gathering the bouquet.

"My sister is arriving in town today. She..."

Abraham did not care to stand around and listen to grownup talk, so he stuffed both hands into his pockets and darted off in the direction of the beach. If mother said she was not worried about Bullebak or Nixies, then neither was he.

Netherlands, 1864

The Doctor had not been prepared for the physical toll of cleaning the fishermen's bodies from the beach, and his arms ached. The rare sunny day in Amsterdam made the task more brutal than if they'd been afforded a merciful layer of cloud, but in the end, he sewed the men back together as best he could, wrapped them in clean white cloths and helped heave them onto the wagon to take to the morgue. There was no removing the sand that stuck to their injuries, no way to make them appear well enough for an open casket service, even with all the tools of a mortician, but at least they could be put to rest somewhat whole. As the gulls picked at the ruby morsels of meat and tendon left unsalvaged, and the tide began to swell, the moon was rising in a fading sky as the Doctor readied a small boat. He could not stop himself from calling to memory the details of the day he met the Bullebak, the day he learned that it is not a cruel nature that ripped those men apart this day, but a vengeful one, a righteous one. A nature that is more loyal than any man the Doctor had met.

Netherlands, 1836

Abraham sprinted to the beach, holding his pocket gingerly so that it wouldn't jostle. Brine enveloped the air, the rhythmic rush and crash of waves grew louder, and then came the commotion of mariners with their boats docked, hands at the bases of their fish knives. There were four little divots in the sand where the drowned children had been dragged and placed ashore the day before.

One of the fishermen, who appeared to be around eighteen, spotted Abraham and started waving his arms.

"Off! Off the beach! It isn't safe for children!"

Abraham peered up from beneath his copper lashes.

"I only want to play a little."

"Absolutely not! No playing here today! Didn't you see the fliers? There's a monster on the loose! We are planning to find it and kill it. So, you run along now, go back to your parents."

The man returned to the group of young fishermen, all yelling over each other about how best to pursue their crusade, their eyes gleaming with anticipated bravado. Abraham turned to slink away, when a sound like the tenor of a Gregorian monk floated over the clamor of conspiracy and the constancy of waves. Abraham looked back to see whether the fishermen were as baffled by the sound as he was, but they seemed not to notice it, even as the voice vibrated Abraham's bones, beckoning him closer.

He walked toward the voice, through the grey-green brushes of beach grass, which climbed over his head. When the men were out of sight, and the voice was nearer, he emerged from the greenery and approached the water. The waves started to recede, as if the ocean were drying up, creating a pathway of spongey sand and tiny, burrowing clams. A knee-high yet gradually lengthening wall of water on either side of him shivered and flowed within itself.

Abraham followed the path, that voice moving through his blood, filling his throat with song. There was a cave ahead that sparkled like rough amethyst. Its entryway, appearing pitch black in the glare of the sun, seemed to swallow all the light of day. Abraham crossed into its shadow, the temperature dropping so low that if he could see at all, his breath would appear as vapor.

Abraham shivered, and the singing stopped, replaced by wet, raspy breathing. The heady, metallic scent of fish guts and the rust of human blood filled his nostrils. Abraham pushed deeper into the cave and stepped on something—a slingshot. Whatever was in there with him opened its eyes, and they glowed as brightly as two yellow lamps, with dark, sinuous pupils that seemed to swirl like a river. The eyes themselves illuminated a maw with many long, wet teeth and bluish skin marked with little wounds dripping a strange, silvery plasma. Abraham scooped up the slingshot and the creature screeched, the once sonorous song replaced with a scraping wail that reverberated off the walls.

The creature rushed Abraham, but a thin snap made it pause just short of his outstretched hands, which held the slingshot, its handle splintered in two. The creature looked at Abraham with something like curiosity, its breath slowing, its claws chittering. Abraham dropped the broken slingshot, reached into his pocket and pulled out a largely intact eggshell, setting it on the ground between them. The thing bent low to look at it, and Abraham smiled, when the great crack of an explosion erupted behind him. The creature crumpled in on itself and fell forward, crushing the eggshell into splintering pieces. Abraham's ears rang, filled with a pressure like being plunged underwater, and then the group of fishermen swarmed around him, hooting and hollering, praising Abraham for leading them to the creature's lair. One of them twirled a smoking, golden flintlock on his finger, and another lifted Abraham into his arms.

The child's eyes streamed. He craned his neck to look back into the cave, wondering why the walls of water hadn't crashed down and drowned them all, when two small, glowing yellow eyes with undulating pupils blinked at him through the darkness. It was all alone.

When the men returned with Abraham to the beach, the water overtook the path, and the cave was once again swallowed by the sea. Something had allowed him to leave safely.

Netherlands, 1864

The Doctor rowed himself, alone, onto the calm, glassy surface of the sea. He had never seen the sea so still. Though he had not returned to this beach since he was a child, he remembered where the cave had been, like it had been mapped into the palm of his hand, a place revealed by an otherworldly tide and hanging in his mind like a nightmare. It would be underwater now, but when he arrived where he was sure he would find the Bullebak, he began to sing in that same deep tone he had heard when he was a child. He could not achieve the same note exactly, but hoped that in the dark and quiet, the creature would recognize the tune of what must have been its mother.

Nothing happened.

"Come out, Bullebak," he said. "Reveal yourself!"

Nothing happened.

The Doctor pulled from his breast pocket a perfectly intact eggshell, only a pinprick hole at its top and bottom where he had blown its contents clean out. The gentle, almost imperceptible waves lapped along the sides of the boat, the surface of the water glinting like onyx in the moonlight. The Doctor pulled his woolen cloak more tightly around his neck.

"When I was small," he said to no one, "I wanted to bring an eggshell to the sea. I wished to meet a witch. It is said that one must break their eggs thoroughly at breakfast, lest a witch should take it, and use it to sail the sea. 'Why?' I thought when I was a boy, 'What's wrong with a witch using my eggshell?'"

Only the water responded, panting a mist that hung in the air.

"I wanted so badly to meet a witch. Or a Nixie, or a Bullebak, for that matter. I loved monsters," he wiped his dripping nose with a gloved hand. The egg wobbled where it sat on the edge of the boat. "I was fascinated by them. I still am," he chuckled. "But things have changed a little."

The water began to undulate; the boat rocked, and the egg rolled into the ocean where it bobbed like a lure. Then two great, glowing yellow eyes emerged from the black depths, followed by a wide mouth with dagger-like teeth and a flowing mane of liquid hair cascading from a light green head. The creature's claws and teeth were stained dark with the blood of the fishermen, the same ones who had killed its mother.

"Hello, Bullebak," said Abraham. "I am Doctor Van Helsing now. I am sorry about what happened to your mother all those years ago."

The Bullebak stared, unblinking, its slithering, living pupils observing the Doctor's every micro expression.

"Those children had been flinging rocks at you, hadn't they? And your mother took the attacks for you and was angry. And those fishermen, you were angry with them. Now you are bigger, and stronger than they, and so you sought to teach them a final lesson, didn't you? Can you understand me?"

The Bullebak twitched one bloodstained claw. It could kill Abraham Van Helsing as quickly as that gun had killed its mother. All it had to do was lunge.

"There is a lifelong feud between man and beast," said Abraham, "and it will only end when one of our species ends."

He reached, slowly, for the revolver holstered at his side. The Bullebak was so transfixed by his words, so absorbed by Abraham's blue eyes never glancing away that it did not notice—or if it did, trusted the Doctor would not harm it. The little eggshell floated between them.

"I am sorry for that," he continued, "for these misunderstandings, for these...instances of bloodshed. You know, men kill *each other*, too. Sometimes for no real reason. Not vengeance, not love. Just because. If there is a difference between your kind and mine, it is this; we kill to kill, and you kill to survive, to protect, to vindicate. I strive to be more like your kind than mine."

In one flash of movement swift as a dying ember, the Doctor whipped out his revolver and shot the Bullebak, the light of its eyes going out like a snuffed candle, its guttural death shriek resounding over the open sea. It flailed, sent sea spray raining down, before sinking in a plume of its own blood under the water and out of sight, overtaken by a bloom of small bubbles. Shark fins already dotted the horizon. Van Helsing holstered his gun and took up his oars, the echo of boyhood sadness tugging at a heart as hollow as an eggshell. He would have cried if he could.

"Forgive me," he whispered, "the cycle had to end with one of us."

As he returned to shore, something crushed the eggshell in one blue, long-taloned hand. Something with two small, glowing yellow eyes. Something that would never forget the face of Doctor Abraham Van Helsing, and that would never forgive. The innocence of youth continued to be drowned by the culling mechanisms of war, and of revenge.

Emily Elledge (she/they) is a writer and wannabe illustrator from Mississippi. She is a stay-at-home mom to one small child and a cat. Her work has been published in *Dracula Beyond Stoker*, *Toad Shade Zine*, and *Jaded Ibis Press*.

Tomb of the Wiedergänger
By Jonathan Maberry

I have been accused of working too much. Reading too much. Thinking too much.

Those accusations are not arrows that miss the target.

It was in the autumn of 1863 that my wife, Katja—and was there ever a woman as lovely and sweet-natured as she? I think not—convinced me to take a holiday. I am not much given to visiting seasides or taking carriage rides through the countryside. Not when there is yet so much to learn about how life works. The mysteries call to me, be it a question of law, a conundrum of philosophy, a question of the unseen world, or a challenge of medical diagnostics. And yet…

Katja has always said I was born with more than an ordinarily serious bent of mind. She is likely correct. Falling in love with her was a surprise to me because I thought myself naturally immune to common tenderness and attachments. Life, as has been said, is rife with wonders, and when she swept into a ballroom during the season in Amsterdam, I was in turn swept off my feet. I even danced, and—as any of my brothers and sisters could tell you factually—I am not a dancer.

Yet I danced with her.

If I ever missed a step, she caught me and steered me toward the right part of the floor, and in doing so steered me toward her innocent heart.

We married a year to the day when we first met, and our son, Koenraad, was born exactly one year later. That date—October 25th—became *our* day. As sacred to us, in its way, as any saint's feast day. Each year we would find some way to celebrate—the ideas always hers, with me following lovestruck in our shared waltz.

At Katja's insistence, we went to Bavaria, where her people still lived in a small town called Weilheim. Koenraad was just five and was her joy. He had been a sickly baby and for a dark few weeks we thought we would lose him to consumption, but it turned out to be a very bad and persistent cold. Once he rallied he was full of vigor and filled with life. It shone from his bright eyes and from the perfect beauty of his smile.

Koenraad often smiled. Every day, and for no reason beyond a pretty leaf falling, a doe seen in the woods, a slanting ray of golden sunlight through a cloudy sky. That kind of simplicity is quite powerful and I thanked God every night and morning for that boy and his mother.

Despite my reluctance to take a holiday, the trip to Bavaria was lovely. The house of Katja's family, less so.

In earlier centuries the Hubers were distant but important cousins to the Von Altendorfs, but bloodlines, like rivers, can change course or dry up. For the Hubers, it was a matter of producing daughters but few sons. A wiser patriarch or more socially-aware matriarch might have managed better marriages for those girls, but alas, with each generation the family fortunes dwindled. Lands were sold off, tenants moved away, and taxes became crippling. Now Herrenhaus von Huber was a crumbling pile that was being slowly and surely devoured by ivy, mold, and decay.

With all that, the rooms were large, the fireplaces ablaze with crackling warmth, and the meals quite excellent. With fewer people living on the land, the game was plentiful, and the ancient cook whose family had been with the Hubers for three hundred years knew her trade as well as anyone from Berlin or Munich.

For Koenraad, the estate was a wonderland of discovery. And the lad was everywhere at once. I swear there were a dozen of him at any time. Climbing a tree to peer into birds' nests, foraging for truffles out near the pond, digging for buried treasure in the kitchen garden—and finding mostly chicken bones and some old pieces of broken pottery. He had his mother's honest innocence and—I say this with equal measures of pride and humility—his father's inquisitive mind. I was already a polymath by then and he was demonstrably more observant than I had been at his age. I had no doubt he would grow to be a man of learning and deep understanding.

Katja spent much of her time with her cousins, all of them women. They ranged in age from young Gertrude, who was fifteen and already thinking about who she might marry, to the eldest, Hilde, who was widow at forty and, alas, eleven years of grief had aged her to a wrinkled crone. The master of the house was Heinrich, who seemed perpetually confused about the numbers—and names—of all the women in his house. When I asked my wife as to her uncle's age, she laughed and said, "Oh, he was probably on the Ark with Noah." And, indeed, he looked to be that old. A tall, gaunt, stooped old gentleman who spoke mainly to himself and avoided crowded sitting rooms.

There were servants and dogs and even a pair of feral cats who had been brought in the previous winter and now lived in the kitchen, claiming it as their own little kingdom. They prowled the manor at night and kept themselves well-fed on rats and mice, and therefore earned their place.

We settled down for a quiet month of peace and happiness.

Alas, that peace did not thrive in Weilheim.

Alas, that happiness did not dwell there.

It was on the 19th of October—our sixth day as residents of Herrenhaus von Huber, when we decided on an outing. We took the family's dog cart along country lanes. Katja and

Koenraad headed off to visit some old ruins in the woods east of the house. At a crossroads I leapt down with a net bag, a butterfly net, and many small jars. My form of relaxation was to wander the fields that had now grown fierce and wild, carrying with me a list of herbs I thought to collect for use in my medical studies. I blew kisses to my wife and son, and watched them roll away, Koenraad singing a nursery rhyme for which he had composed new lyrics about talking trees.

I felt very blessed and stood watching until they were out of sight. Then I turned and focused my mind on those things that enchanted my scientific mind.

One of my teachers had been the German chemist Carl Friedrich Wilhelm Meissner who, among other things, was a natural philosopher who made a particular study of naturally-occurring compounds he labeled 'alkaloids.' I was fascinated by his writings, and those of Oscar Jacobson and Albert Ladenberg. Some gentlemen may have preferred an afternoon of shooting or lawn sports, but I found delight in discovering what secrets were held by the Earth itself and nature in its endless generosity.

For the next few hours I hunted for, and found, many healthy specimens. There was stinging nettle—useful for easing pain in the joints and as a treatment for anemia—and arnica, which was powerful when made into a salve for pain relief and wounds. I found yellow gentian which, despite its bitter taste, was an excellent aid to digestion and was often named in pharmacopeias as a base for medicines. There was yarrow, also useful for digestion, and soothing chamomile. Dandelion abounded, and I gathered enough for some experiments I had in mind focused on detoxification. And more—lemon balm, sanicula, and mint.

It was the hunt for alpine rose that brought me to a brook of clear water. Although it was the middle of autumn, the day was hot and the briskly tumbling water promised to soothe my feet, which had become sore after climbing up and down the hills. I removed my shoes and stockings and sat down on a rock with my feet in the brook, and lit a pipe. I was sure Heaven itself had no more enchanting moments as that one. A rabbit came to the far side of the water to drink and we regarded each other kindly, he in his world and me in mine, at a place where those worlds overlapped.

As I tapped the dottle from my pipe bowl, I heard a sound and looked up to see a man standing on the far side of the brook from me, a distance of perhaps twenty feet. To my astonishment, though, he was not dressed in country clothes, nor even city dress. Instead he wore a heavy, ankle-length overcoat of waxed leather, breeches from an entirely different century, boots, waxed gloves, a wide-brimmed hat, and an arrangement of thick glass lenses held in place by a buckled band. He leaned on a tall staff, and upon his face there was a grotesque mask with an extended bird's beak.

He was clad in the singular garb of a plague doctor from the days of the Black Death. I must admit that I both started and even cried out in my surprise. Then, quickly recollecting myself, coughed to clear my constricted throat and got to my feet. I offered a quick bow to this enigmatic person.

"Good afternoon," I said. "Forgive me, but I did not hear you approach."

He stood unspeaking for a handful of seconds, observing me with eyes but half-seen through colored lenses.

"I apologize for being startled," I said into that silence. "And please forgive me for being uncouth, but I wonder at your costume. Is there a celebration of some kind in the neighborhood?"

The man looked off to the east for a moment. Before turning back to face me, he spoke in a voice that was leaden and dull, as if speaking his thoughts aloud and to himself.

"Have you seen the *wiedergänger*?"

I smiled. "I beg your pardon, but…*wiedergänger*? Re-walker…? I do not grasp the meaning of that word."

Instead of answering, he said, "The dead are near." His face was still turned to the east.

"Ah," I said, believing I understood both his question and his costume. "Yes, there is a cemetery not three miles from here, and it adjoins what is called the *Pestkapelle*—the Weilheim Plague Chapel."

At those words he turned sharply toward me. "What do you know of that place?"

I felt I was being tested, perhaps as part of some arcane local custom. We have our own idiosyncratic ways in the Netherlands, and some are quite odd, so it was not surprising that rural Bavaria would have its own. This fellow could be some kind of story-keeper for the region, dressing up in such an outlandish fashion to coincide with certain holidays.

To respect his little drama, I fished in my head for what I knew. But that was no labor, for had not Old Heinrich mentioned it over brandy and cigars not two days past?

I said, "There was an outbreak of plague here in the fall and winter of 1633 into 1634. During the Thirty Years' War. It is believed that it came to this place with soldiers marching to war. That outbreak took the lives of nearly a third of the residents of the town, as I seem to recall. Fearing a worse catastrophe, the dead were taken from the town in carts and buried in mass graves beneath where the chapel now stands, with the nobles of the land interred in the Huber family crypt. In the last century, an ossuary was constructed and the remains of the dead citizens placed there. I believe there is a fresco of Saint Roch there to watch over the victims of that tragedy."

I paused and gave him a hopeful smile.

"Are my facts correct, sir? And is that what you meant by *wiedergänger?* That the dead have *moved* from one grave to another?"

I wasn't quite sure what kind of reply I expected. Laughter at my expense, which I, a stranger to that part of the world, would have accepted with good grace. Or perhaps a didactic clarification of any of my errors.

But in both assumptions I was mistaken. His hand seemed to tighten on his staff, and in a sharp tone he said, "You know nothing."

By this point my patience was beginning to erode. I do not mind a joke or even to have my leg pulled, but good manners impose some limits on such things.

With a touch of asperity I replied, "I know only what the master of Herrenhaus von Huber, who is my uncle by marriage, has told me, and as these are his lands I must defer to his knowledge."

The plague doctor merely stared at me but used his free hand to gesture toward Weilheim. "Do you actually believe that the plague of death is over? For I know it is not."

"Surely," I said, "you know that this is untrue. I may not be a local resident but I know my medical history well enough. There have been three outbreaks of the Black Death this century. The earliest ran from 1812 to 1816 in Egypt in parts of the Ottoman Empire, though there are some credible reports, particularly from Crete, that said there were deaths as late as 1839. Then in 1813 into 1814, there was a more severe outbreak in in the Balkans, and another in Majorca in 1820. We are decades past those and very many miles from those places. If anyone has died of illness around here, then it is likely those diseases common to farming communities."

The plague doctor once more turned his face toward Weilheim. "The dead are restless, and they are lonely," he said, once more in that distant and introspective tone.

"Restless? Lonely?" I echoed. "May I ask what you mean by this?"

"They crave the warmth of the living," he said, shaking his head slowly. "Breath and blood. Nothing else can ease the pain of the cold, cold grave."

"At the risk of offending, I must say that such a statement is either a joke or fanciful rubbish. Death is the end of life. Except, perhaps, for the immortal spirit rising to judgment or falling to punishment. In terms of an earthly presence, the dead are dead and that is an end to it."

Now he gave me another hard look. "Think you so?" He spat into the running waters. "What do *you* know of death?"

"I am a medical man," I said. "A physician from Amsterdam. I can say with some certainty that the phenomenon of death is very much in my purview."

"But do you know what the dead crave?" The stranger laughed, bitter and cold. "They are jealous, are the dead. They see what is denied to them and they covet it. Breath and blood. Ware those who step too close to where the *wiedergänger* sleep, for they are ever hungry and sleep but lightly."

"What does all this mean, sir?" I demanded.

"It means that death covets what you take for granted." Then he gestured toward Weilheim and crossed himself.

I blinked and then started, for in that miniscule fragment of time the man dressed as the plague doctor vanished entirely. I splashed across the brook but could not even find his footprints. Nonplussed, I stood there, doubting my senses and my sanity.

I had just begun to convince myself that I had fallen asleep while sitting on my stone and that all of this was a strange dream. And then, carried on the wind, came a sound that chilled me to the bone.

It was a scream.

And I knew it for the scream of my own beloved Katja.

I ran.

G od in his heaven, how I ran. Without pausing to put on my shoes, I ran up the slope and across the fields and through dense stands of trees. Calling her name, I ran.

The screams grew louder as I grew closer, and there was a quality in her cries that threatened to unman me. It was not merely the shock and panic that ignites any scream, but there was a note of hysteria. Or worse.

And so I ran as if the world behind me was on fire.

I cut across country, eschewing the road, and that cut my journey in half, though every second felt as long as a century. And the screams went on and on and on.

Then I spotted the dog cart standing in the road outside of the Pestkapelle. The Plague Crypt. The horse was skittish and kept tossing his head and stamping the ground, clearly terrified of something.

The screams were fading as I drew near. The intensity had become resignation of some horror but there was no longer a pleading note. No longer were the screams calling for help. Instead, to my despair, they sounded now like a terrible acceptance.

I dashed through the iron gate and into the crypt, and then I skidded to a stop as my own screams tried to claw their way out of my chest.

There was Katja, sitting on the lowest step of a dais on which a coffin sat that was made from stone, with a heavy marble slab atop it. She held Koenraad in her arms and sat there rocking back and forth. Her screams crumpled into moans that sounded if they were pulled from the lowest chamber of her soul.

Our child lay limp in her arms. Katja kept lifting his head and pushing his slack lips toward her breast as if encouraging him to suckle.

But Koenraad was far beyond such things.

The soft, pale flesh of my son was savagely torn and the skin glistened with bright red. Katja heard me gasp and she looked at me with eyes that were too wide and too bright.

"Katja! What has happened?" I cried. "Who has done this? My God, Katja, what happened to our son?"

"Abraham," she said as if this were any other day and not the end of our world, "we called for you but you did not come. Our baby called your name, as did I. But you did not come. You did not."

"Who *did* this?"

There was one moment of a stinging clarity as her eyes met mine with shocking force. "Ware those who step too close to where they sleep, for they are ever hungry and sleep but lightly."

They were the same words spoken by the plague doctor. Then, the brightness of shock disintegrated into something else. She began laughing.

God and all his angels, that laugh!

It was a sound born in hell and forged in the fires of complete anguish. It was a laugh from which all sanity was absent. And in her eyes I saw to my horror that something within her had broken. Completely and utterly shattered.

I do not even recall how I got Katja and Koenraad into the dog cart. There was no memory of the drive back to the manor except for the continual howl of insane laughter. That is a memory I will take to my grave.

I must have screamed myself for as we closed on the house people poured out. Her sisters and cousins. Her uncle. The gamekeeper and cook and butler. They came running, and as each saw what ghastly burden lay wrapped in Katja's arms, they cried out. Hands reached for us. Katja fought with feral viciousness as they tried to take Koenraad from her.

Perhaps I helped. I do not remember. A veil of blackness had fallen across my eyes and my next clear memory was of sitting beside a bed on which Katja lay, still clutching the still and silent form of our child.

For a day and a night Katja sat with Koenraad. I sat with her, trying to calm her, to soothe her, but I do not think she was even truly aware of me. She spoke in a singsong to the boy as if he were a little baby again.

I managed to get a potent sleeping draught into her and, when she finally slept, we took the body. Her sisters helped me bear him to a different room and there I was finally able to make my first clear examination of that dreadful wound. The flesh was torn, and it took all of the strength I possessed and every ounce of clinical control I could summon to use my fingers to press the ragged skin back into place. There I saw what was hidden by the ugliness of the injury.

There were two round holes. Punctures, with the edges of flesh pushed into each wound. They were not marks that any knife would make, nor were they accidental injuries from Katja's brooch.

No, these were more like the marks of teeth. A dog at least, or perhaps a wolf. There was some residual bruising revealed while sponging away the blood. Those bruises were long and slender and clearly made by the fingers of strong, clasping hands.

I sagged back.

"My son was *murdered.*"

Gertrude, Katja's eldest sister, stepped back from the bed and crossed herself. Then she clutched the small silver crucifix that hung on a chain around her neck, kissed the feet of the savior, and pressed the talisman to her chest. As she did this, she spoke a single word.

"*Wiedergänger.*"

Anger nearly overtook me and I had to fight to keep strong words from my mouth. In as calm a voice as I could manage, I said, "Rubbish. He was attacked by a dog. A wolf at most."

Gertrude gave me a look that was half heartbreak and half pity. "I will send for the priest." That was all she said before fleeing.

I spent hours in the manor's library, searching for any reference to *wiedergänger* among the volumes of local lore. There were a few but they were obscure and none of the scholars seemed able to agree on exactly what a 're-walker' was. The oldest writings dated back to the time of the Black Death and some of the entries bordered on the hysterical, claiming that the land was cursed and that anyone who died by violence or suicide would rise from their own graves to prey on the living.

Naturally I found this to be absurd. Silly, even, though it offended me that priests of bygone centuries played upon the credulity of their parishioners in so hideous a fashion.

Some of the books referenced other supposedly supernatural beings who were also believed to be spirits of the dead who found sustenance in things they took from living people. Blood was very common, but others fed on breath, on hope, even on faith. Some, like the *nachzehrer*, were flesh-eaters. The other monsters in these lurid accounts included the *alp* and the *nuentoter.*

I tossed the books aside and sank back into a chair, feeling grief and pain rise up like a great wave inside my chest.

When the village priest arrived, he gave last rites to my son and then prayed while standing over Katja's bed. He, too, tried to tell me of the danger of monsters rising from the grave. He spoke of how to combat such creatures—including the use of rosewood stakes, a presentation of the Holy Eucharist, placement of the flowers and bulbs of the garlic plant, and the church's own Ritual of Exorcism, which included beheading the corpse of a *wiedergänger's* victim, filling the mouth with garlic, then using rosewood or iron to pin the body inside the coffin to prevent it from rising.

I thanked him but sent him away, having no time for such foolishness.

Would that he had stayed.

We buried Koenraad in the Huber family crypt because I had no estate back in Amsterdam appropriate for so precious an interment. Katja could not attend. She was lost to me, her mind broken, her thoughts straying into lands of shadow, perhaps looking for the soul of our child.

I remained at the manor for some weeks, trying everything in my power to ease her suffering, but, as I said…she was lost. The priest visited often and on one trip brought with him some of the things he spoke of, fearing that this might be the kind of unearthly attack he feared. He gave me a long rosewood cane whose end was sharpened to a point, and with it a bottle of holy water mixed with oil of garlic. He bade me wear the crucifix and to keep the bottle in my pocket. I did that much to humor him, but ended that conversation.

Then, a month after the funeral, the entire house was awakened by the most horrifying of screams coming from Katja's room. I was closest and ran to her, bursting in and then stopping in my tracks. Gertrude lay insensible on the floor and Katja was sitting up, her eyes wide and vacant but a smile on her lips.

And there, crouching over her and bent to suckle blood from a gash on her breast was…

My god, how can I even write the words? How could this be true? How, in the world God made, could such things even be possible?

There, lapping up the fresh blood like a dog, was Koenraad.

He was dressed in the clothes in which we buried him. His hands were white as wax but his face glowed with health and life as he drank and drank.

What could any sane man do in such a moment? Join my wife in the comfort of madness? Open my own veins to feed this *thing* that wore the face and form of my beloved child? Our only child?

I prayed that God would strike me down there and then so that I did not have to witness a moment more of this. And to prevent me from doing those wretched things the priest told me of.

"Koenraad," I said, and he looked up from his feast. His face was that of my beloved child—sweet and handsome and innocent—but his eyes…

God in Heaven, his eyes.

They were the color of the blood that smeared his mouth. A dark red that seemed as hot as hell's flames. Even so, what was worse was his smile. With his mother's blood on his lips, he grinned at me like a jackal. Worse. Like a demon.

"Father," he said softly. "Mother is so delicious. Will you not feast with me and then we can all live forever."

I felt my own mind beginning to tear apart. In that moment I was not Abraham Van Helsing, the student of science, the reasonable man. No. He died in that room. Instead, I heard myself roar out like a lion, like a bear. I felt myself move without knowing I even could. With quick steps I closed on him, one hand tearing the crucifix from around my neck and with the other clawing the bottle from my pocket.

Koenraad saw these things and doubt flickered in his crimson eyes. Perhaps being what he now was—this *wiedergänger*—gifted him with knowledge known only to the damned. Or perhaps he saw the rage that filled me to bursting.

I shoved the cross at him and he recoiled, hissing like a cat. Even then my heart tried to convince my mind that this was a child reacting in understandable fear. However, his clothes were what we *buried* him in.

Then I used my teeth to pull the cork from the little vial of blessed water and garlic oil. At the first scent of the garlic, Koenraad shrank away, shoving Katja roughly toward me as a barrier.

"You are not my son," I cried and snapped my hand forward so that the oil splashed him across the face and the palms of his upraised hands. Instantly that unblemished skin erupted into red blisters, and as these swelled and popped, smoke rose that stank of burned meat and decay.

He tried to fight me, but each time he lunged toward me the crucifix forced him back and the holy water and garlic burned him. Over and over again until he whirled, ran toward the window, and leapt out into the night. I rushed over and to my astonished eyes saw that it was not his body falling but that of a monstrous bat rising into the night and flapping off toward the family crypt.

I dared not follow him into the night. Not even armed with those sacred things.

Instead I turned back to Katja, whose eyes were still open. Had she seen? Did she understand? I fear I will never know, for her mind now wandered in some unknown country from which there was no return.

I gathered her to me and held her, rocking her the way she rocked with Koenraad that day. My words came out in a tumble as I swore on my own immortal soul that I would not let Koenraad suffer as a creature of darkness.

I wept as I said these words, and knew that from that moment on there would always be a part of me on guard, armed with the tools of this new, strange war.

Always.

In the morning, I headed toward the crypt. I had with me the crucifix and what was left of the oil. I had a hatchet tucked into my belt and carried in my hand the rosewood stake.

I will not write down what I did to the body of he who had been my son. It is enough to say that he is at peace. He is with God.

As for Katja, she lives now forever in an asylum in Amsterdam. She is well-cared for and I visit as often as my broken heart will allow.

And me?

I have become a doctor and a metaphysician. I teach my students and do my research and I try to be alive. At night I listen for the flap of wings. I search shadows for red eyes and white teeth.

There is a war ongoing, and in my own way I have become a soldier in that war.

Now…and forever.

Jonathan Maberry is a NYTimes bestselling author, 5-time Bram Stoker Award-winner, 4-time Scribe Award winner, Inkpot Award winner, editor, writing teacher, poet, playwright, and comic book writer. He writes in multiple genres including thriller, horror, sci-fi, mystery, and fantasy. V-WARS (Netflix) was based on his books/comics; Alcon is developing his Rot & Ruin novels for film; and Chad Stahelski, director of *JOHN WICK,* is developing his Joe Ledger thrillers for TV. Marvel's *BLACK PANTHER: WAKANDA FOREVER* was partly based on his work. He's written more than 55 novels, 200 short stories, 30 graphic novels, 1200 feature articles, and two dozen nonfiction books. Jonathan has also edited nearly 30 anthologies, including *Aliens, The X-Files,* the official tribute to *Scary Stories to Tell in the Dark,* and many others. He's the president of the International Association of Media Tie-in Writers, and the editor of Weird Tales Magazine. www.jonathanmaberry.com

Papers More
By Brandon Keaton

Amsterdam, November 1876.

By the time the corpse lifted its hand, half the jury were already inclined to acquit. The right hand, which had lain palm down on the sheet, turned itself palm-up by two inches. The inquest room had been built for drafts, not visibility; the high windows gave a flat gray light, and the glass between the room and the mortuary reflected more of the jurymen's faces than the dead man's.

Only Professor Abraham Van Helsing had his eyes on the dead.

He watched the finger uncurl with the practiced detachment of a man who has seen worse things in better lighting. The wrist lay at the exact angle in which he had placed it an hour before; no twitching, no convulsion, no consoling clench.

The skin, though, troubled him. It ought, by now, to have taken on a respectable wax of death. Instead, it kept a faint but stubborn warmth of tone, like cooled candlewax that has not yet decided whether to harden.

A fly that had blundered in from the canal buzzed three hopeful circles over the slab, then made an abrupt turn in the air rather than landing.

"In all relevant respects," the magistrate was saying, "the body being, ah—" He squinted down at the paper in his hand. "'not yet dead.' Is that your phrasing, Professor?"

The room's attention swung to Van Helsing. Twelve jurymen examined him as if he were the specimen. The defense advocate, a young man with a fashionable beard, brightened. The prosecutor's left eyebrow climbed toward heaven.

Van Helsing closed his notebook, and stood to his feet.

"It is, mijnheer," he said. "Though I had not anticipated hearing it in open court."

A ripple of amusement moved through the benches. Even the widow—Liane De Groot, twenty-nine, head to toe in black—looked up, startled, as if humor were a thing unfamiliar.

"This is an *inquest*, Professor, not a faculty meeting," the magistrate snapped. "Plain words are better than Latin." He tapped the paper. "You have written that the deceased is 'in all respects, save one, dead,' and that 'in the remaining respect the question is open.' The court would much be obliged if you would explain what that is supposed to mean."

"In law," Van Helsing said mildly. "It means I am giving the court the benefit of the doubt."

The prosecutor made a sound that might have been a cough or a laugh. The defense advocate's mustache twitched.

"In medicine," Van Helsing went on, "it means the functions by which we commonly recognise life are suspended, yet some signs persist which, if they belong solely to the living, we should not hesitate to call vital. Warmth of the skin, freshness of the eye, et cetera. The absence of—" he inclined his head toward the mortuary door, "certain stenches I have spared the clerk."

The clerk, who had been bracing for what came next, finally relaxed.

"So." The magistrate feigned a smile, as if sensing what might be hiding between the lines. "You are asking this court to consider the possibility that the late Willem De Groot is both dead and not dead."

"Such words could also describe our Lord and Savior, yes?" Van Helsing shot back.

A murmur ran around the room. De Groot's widow pressed her handkerchief over her mouth.

"I am asking the court," Van Helsing said, "to consider intermediate conditions our statutes have not yet defined. There are already legal fictions for such things. We declare a man dead when he has not been seen for seven years, though a body is never produced. We name the unborn capable of inheritance. If the law can make room for the invisible and the not-yet, it can find words for the not-*quite*."

The air in the room changed. The jury, who had trudged in expecting to rubber-stamp a domestic tragedy, sat a little straighter.

"Professor," the magistrate said, "this court has no intention of setting a precedent. Did Liane De Groot kill her husband, or did she not? Your report complicates that question. You have written that the marks on his neck are 'consistent with cutting or biting, and conclusive of nothing.' And then you add this." He read: "'If the body should exhibit movement post-mortem, it would be prudent, for the avoidance of doubt, to treat it as not yet dead.'"

Behind the glass, on the slab, Willem De Groot lay still under his sheet, the outline of his shoulders just discernible. His right hand remained palm-up, as if inviting argument.

"Tell us, Professor, what *movement* might you have in mind?"

"In my experience," Van Helsing said, "movement of the eyes, the mouth, and hands are the most likely to distress lay witnesses. A convulsion of the limbs, the sudden opening of the eyes, a reaching gesture—these can be explained as the final discharge of nerves. Yet if you do not expect them, you may say very unhelpful things under oath."

A few of the jurymen smiled; one crossed himself with his index finger.

"Professor," the defense advocate said, seizing his chance, "are we to understand that there is a possibility—however remote—that my client's husband may resume his former condition?"

Twelve jurymen leaned forward. De Groot's widow dropped her handkerchief.

Van Helsing, who had in fact seen a man resume his former condition in a cemetery near Rotterdam—and had slept badly ever since—smiled in a way he hoped looked reassuring.

"The late Willem De Groot has no former condition to resume which would be agreeable to this court," he said.

A wave of laughter quickly stifled.

"Nevertheless," Van Helsing added, "until the question is closed, I advise that he be treated as not yet dead."

At that moment, the fly returned. It hovered over the sheet, dipped toward the face beneath, and then dropped like a stone, landing on its back with its legs in the air.

Van Helsing opened his notebook calmly, and wrote: *The insects, too.*

Then he underlined a phrase which, years later, he would wish he had never set down in ink:

Not yet dead.

The night prior to the inquest, the mortuary was colder than the Prinsengracht. They had given Van Helsing a key, which he suspected was a clerical error; professors were supposed to knock and wait while someone fetched the right ledger. The lock turned easily, and when it opened, smells older than stone and damp linen met him.

"Professor?" the attendant called. "We weren't expecting you until tomorrow."

"I'm afraid I'm seized," Van Helsing said, "with an unprofessional desire to be thorough."

Visser emerged, gray and narrow, wiping his hands on his apron. "They say you're both doctor and lawyer. Is this one going to court?"

"If I have anything to say about it," Van Helsing said, "he will go nowhere at all."

The body of Willem De Groot lay on the slab. The gas lamp above them hissed as Van Helsing set down his bag and laid out thermometer, notebook, and spectacles. When he lifted the sheet, the dead man's face looked as all cruel faces do when emptied out:

smaller, the malice gone from the eyes but still lingering about the mouth.

"Has he been identified?" he asked.

"Six hours ago. The wife didn't seem upset," Visser said.

"That is not yet evidence," Van Helsing replied. "Only taste."

He began with the usual things. Temperature. Rigor—or the lack of it. He spoke aloud as he went, and Visser repeated the readings after him.

"No stiffness in the limbs," Van Helsing said. "Too free for so many hours." He lifted one eyelid. The green eye beneath was still clear. "Eyes too bright. Lids not gummy. No odor yet." He sniffed, to be certain.

The wounds on the neck were worse than the widow's account had indicated: two neat punctures above the clavicle, crescent-shaped bruising around them. When Van Helsing cleaned them, a thin ooze of dark blood welled up.

"Still fluid," he said. "Hmm."

He laid his palm flat on the bare chest. The heart kept no beat, and there was warmth that had no business being there. He had felt such warmth once before, in Leiden. That time he'd made the mistake of waiting to see what it would do.

"Cause of death?" Visser prompted.

"Write: 'Syncope from loss of blood, pending inquest.' Leave a space. The night may have further opinions."

Visser went away muttering, and Van Helsing took out his notebook and began to write. Name, date, descriptors of the man, old scars, new bruises. *Lesions consistent with a narrow double-pointed instrument or with human teeth*, he wrote. *Conclusive of nothing*. Nothing, he thought, that I can name twice.

The lamp sputtered. Something tickled the back of his neck.

A fly had found its way in. It circled the length of the slab—above the knees, the open shirt—and veered away each time it came near the skin of the throat.

"For completeness," Van Helsing said, "one housefly, reluctant."

He did not write that down.

"In all relevant respects," he wrote instead, "the body may be regarded as dead."

Relevant steadied him. It was a lawyer's word. In his experience, the law had always been generous to the dead and suspicious of the living.

"In one respect," he went on, "the question remains open."

He listed the irregularities: warmth, delayed staining, clarity of the eyes, oozing of blood. Each on its own might be dismissed. Together, they made a pattern that he recognized.

At the bottom of the page, he hesitated, then finished his sentence with: "it would be prudent, for the avoidance of doubt, to treat it as not yet dead."

Those last four words sat on the paper like a loaded weapon. He almost scratched them out. Instead, he underlined *prudent*. Another lawyer's word. One that magistrates liked; it committed them only toward caution.

"Professor?" Visser called from the doorway. "Any further need of me?"

"Only to lock the door," Van Helsing said. "And to tell anyone who follows that the body's not to be touched until the court orders otherwise."

"Some folk dislike the body to lie unblessed overnight," Visser said. "The wife asked about bringing a priest."

Van Helsing looked down at De Groot's face. In the lamplight, the lips seemed a fraction ruddier than before.

"She may come," he said. "The priest may not."

He signed the report, folded it for the clerk, and slipped it into his bag.

A faint sound from the slab.

Not a convulsion, not the jolt of a settling joint; a soft, deliberate exhalation, as if the man sighed into cupped hands. Van Helsing laid two fingers where the pulse would be if De Groot had any business left with pulses.

Nothing. Only that stubborn, persisting warmth.

"You," he said softly, "are not yet dead."

He pulled the sheet back over the face, took the key from inside the door, and locked the mortuary from the outside.

The jurymen no longer stared at Liane De Groot as if she were the whole problem; their gazes moved between Van Helsing, the magistrate, and the glass that separated them from the mortuary.

"The court is grateful for your prudence, Professor. You may sit," the magistrate said. "Unless counsel has further questions."

"If it please the court," the prosecutor said, "I should like the professor to clarify the matter of the neck wounds."

Van Helsing remained standing.

"The marks are," the prosecutor consulted his notes, "consistent with cutting or biting and conclusive of nothing. Yet you do not rule out that they were inflicted by human teeth?"

"I do not," Van Helsing said.

"In which case," the prosecutor continued, "they may perfectly well have been inflicted by the deceased's wife in the struggle she *admits* took place."

"The bruising pattern," Van Helsing said, "suggests the deceased was accustomed to delivering blows, not receiving them."

"The pattern also suggests," the prosecutor said smoothly, "that this was not the first quarrel in that house. It is possible that Liane De Groot seized her husband by the throat—" he mimed a twisting motion with both hands "—and committed a grave act in the heat of the moment?"

Liane made a small sound. A whimper.

One of the younger jurymen flinched.

"It is possible," Van Helsing said. "It is also possible that he fell down the stairs. Or that a passing burglar took a liking to his waistcoat. Possibilities are cheap. Evidence is dearer. You brought me here for the latter."

A breath of delight moved through the benches. The magistrate rapped his knuckles on the table.

"Please confine yourself to medicine, Professor."

"I try," Van Helsing said. "The law keeps following."

The defense advocate rose.

"If the court might indulge a possibility of mine," he said. "Professor, is it also possible that these wounds were *self-inflicted?*"

The prosecutor snorted. "What man has teeth to bite his own neck?"

"The sort," the advocate said, "who drinks too much and enjoys frightening his wife. Or who seeks to accuse her in advance." He turned to Van Helsing. "You observed old bruising did you not?"

"Yes."

"And newer ones on my client?"

"Yes."

"Is there any medical reason to suppose," the advocate said, "that a man who has spent years beating his wife might not, on the eve of his death, attempt a new cruelty? To make her appear a murderess?"

The jurymen shifted in their seats. The ginger-haired one stared at Liane as if seeing a woman for the first time.

"As a physician," Van Helsing said, "I can say only that men who injure others seldom refrain from injuring themselves, when it suits them."

"And as a lawyer?"

"We have enough of those," the magistrate cut in. "Your opinions on human nature are not in evidence, Professor."

Another ripple of mirth.

"And as a Christian?" asked a voice from the back.

It was one of the older jurors, a baker by the look of his hands. He seemed surprised to find the room listening to him. "If the body is not yet dead…well…is the soul then still in place? Are we to treat him as a man, or—"

"Juror," the magistrate said, pointing sharply, "this is not a catechism class."

"No, sir," Van Helsing said, "but it is an excellent question."

He met the baker's eyes.

"In the teaching I hold," Van Helsing said, "the soul goes where God wills at the moment of death. What remains is a house with the furniture still in it." He nodded toward the glass. "Sometimes there remains an echo in the rooms."

"Are you sure," the prosecutor said, pouncing, "that what lies in there is only that?"

Across the room, Liane's hands knotted in her lap. Van Helsing thought of the gas-lamp hissing the night before, the long exhalation from Willem's body, the warmth that would not dim.

"In all respects which concern this court," he replied, "yes."

The magistrate inhaled as if to say something brisk in rebuttal. He did not have the chance.

The mortuary door banged open.

Sergeant Mulder strode in without waiting to be called, hat askew.

"Mijnheer," he said to the magistrate, "you told me to report anything unusual at once."

Every head turned toward the glass.

The sheet over Willem De Groot was no longer smooth. It rose in a shallow, unmistakable arc where the chest was, as if something beneath had drawn breath and refused to let it go.

Van Helsing felt the stillness settle over his shoulders like a cloak.

"Well," he said, before panic could ensue, "this seems as good a time as any to be prudent."

The magistrate did not bang his gavel. He did something more alarming: he stood up.

"This inquest," he said, in a voice that had no room for argument, "is adjourned for twenty minutes. Sergeant Mulder, lead the jurymen to the anteroom, then return to guard the defendant. Professor, both counsel—come with me."

Benches scraped; boots shuffled. Liane De Groot half-rose before the clerk's hand on her sleeve stilled her.

Van Helsing followed the magistrate through a side door into his chambers. It was not a grand room: shelves of law reports, a crucifix on the wall, a coal fire brooding in the grate.

"Sit," the magistrate said, but did not.

The prosecutor perched on the edge of a chair while the defense advocate sat with the rapidity of a man glad of furniture. Van Helsing leaned against the wall, so he could see both fire and man.

"Now," said the magistrate. "What, in the name of God, did we just see?"

"A convulsion," the prosecutor said, too quickly. "A late discharge of nervous force. The Professor himself said such things are—"

"What we saw," the magistrate shot back, "was a dead man's chest rise like a bellows full of air and stay there. I have sat on this bench for over fifteen years. I have seen men twitch, grin, empty their bowels after death. I have not seen *that*."

He turned to Van Helsing. "Professor. No Latin. No law. What is this?"

"I think," he said, "that the warning in my report was not superfluous."

"And your recommendation," the magistrate said slowly, "what would it be?"

"I recommend," Van Helsing said, "that the body should be decapitated and burned."

The fire popped.

"Do you seriously wish this court to order a man's head cut off?" the prosecutor asked.

Van Helsing could have said: *Because last time I waited, the body got up.*

"I wish this court," he said, "to use the powers it already has in cases of unusual death and suspected contagion. Section Twelve of the Sanitary Ordinance allows the magistrate to order extraordinary measures whenever the condition of any corpse endangers the living."

"We are not speaking of cholera," the prosecutor protested. "We are speaking of a drunk who died on his own floor."

"We are speaking," Van Helsing said, "of a man who, six hours after death, had not cooled, had not darkened, and now draws breath under a shroud."

"That's impossible," the prosecutor said.

"And yet…" Van Helsing said.

The magistrate's gaze fell upon the crucifix.

"As a Christian," he said slowly, "am I being asked to permit mutilation of a body that may yet contain its soul?"

"As a Catholic," Van Helsing said, "you are being asked to care first for the souls that still unquestionably inhabit their bodies." He spread his hands. "If I am wrong, and this is merely convulsion, we will have dishonored a corpse that can no longer feel it. If I am right, and we do nothing, you will have loosed something which neither law nor Church is prepared to name."

The coal in the fire caved in on itself with a hiss.

"Being a lawyer," the magistrate said, "I am supposed to dislike dilemmas that do not fit the forms."

"You have a statute that fits," Van Helsing said. "You need only be prudent."

The defense advocate huffed. "If the court classifies this as a matter of public health," he said, "then whatever's done to the body is no longer my client's responsibility."

"Wonderful," the prosecutor muttered. "We have invented a new category: homicide by precaution."

"It already exists," Van Helsing said. "You call it quarantine."

"Draft the order," the magistrate said.

"Mijnheer?"

"Write it in your own words, Professor," the magistrate said. "I will sign."

Van Helsing found a certain savage satisfaction in putting the words in precise order. He took up a fresh sheet and wrote, in a neat, dry hand:

> *By virtue of Section XII of the Sanitary Ordinance, and having regard to the unusual condition of the body of Willem De Groot, the court directs that said body be subjected to such measures as Professor Abraham Van Helsing,*

M.D., shall deem necessary for protection of the public; namely, separation of the head from the trunk and the immediate cremation at high heat, to be carried out under official supervision and recorded as a sanitary precaution.

He blotted it and slid it across the desk.

The magistrate read it once, lips moving, then took up his pen.

"For the record," he said, before he signed, "I am doing this as a magistrate."

"As a Christian," Van Helsing said, "you would have done it sooner."

Something like a smile tugged at the magistrate's mouth. He put his name and seal to the order with a hard, practiced stamp.

"You will carry out these measures," he said, pushing the paper back. "With Sergeant Mulder as witness. I shall remain here and pray none of us ever has to explain this to a jury."

Van Helsing folded the order and slipped it into his breast pocket.

"Then, for the avoidance of doubt," he said, "let us make him properly dead."

He opened the door and stepped into the corridor. It seemed longer than it had that morning.

"You are sure, Professor," Sergeant Mulder said, "that this is lawful?"

"I wrote the order," Van Helsing said. "It would be most inconvenient if it were not."

He unlocked the mortuary with the key Visser had given him.

"Visser?" he called.

The attendant appeared from behind a curtain. He had lost what little color he owned.

"I heard you in court," he said. "Is it true? He—"

"You saw it," Van Helsing said.

Visser looked away. "I thought I did. I hoped I was wrong." He swallowed. "After they took you out, I put my hand on him. The chest went down, just like a bellows. Then up again. No heartbeat, though. I checked."

Van Helsing shut the mortuary door behind them and turned the key. The noise sounded final.

"Then we're fortunate," Van Helsing said, "that the city has taken an interest in his breathing."

The sheet over Willem De Groot had settled. The arc at the chest was shallower now, and the fly lay where it had fallen, legs up. There was still no smell of rot.

"Sergeant," Van Helsing said. "You will stand at the head. If there is movement, hold the shoulders. Visser—at the feet, please. Do not speak unless I ask you something. Understood?"

Mulder nodded. Visser nodded with less conviction.

Van Helsing set his bag down and took out what he needed: the narrow trocar he used for draining fluids, the heavy bone saw, the roll of linen. He took a deep breath then folded the sheet back from De Groot's face. The man looked, disconcertingly, better. The cheeks had taken on a faint color; the lips were less bloodless.

Van Helsing laid the back of his hand against the forehead. Warm. Like a fever.

"We must proceed quickly," he said, mostly for Mulder's sake. "If this is only a convulsion, the body will not notice. If it is something else, we'll give it less time to learn."

He bared the chest, locating by touch the space between the ribs where he had gone a hundred times before. The flesh yielded in a way he did not like: not slack, not stiff, but as if something beneath it were reluctant.

"Hold him now," he said.

Mulder's hands tightened on the shoulders. Visser gripped the ankles.

Van Helsing drove the trocar in.

The resistance was brief and then gave with a soft, obscene sigh. The chest heaved up around the steel to meet it. A rush of air fled past Van Helsing's hand, warm and moist, smelling of gin and old meat.

De Groot's eyes shot open.

They did not roll; they did not glaze. They fixed, for one appalling instant, directly on Van Helsing. The lips moved in a small, soundless shape. It might have been Dutch—*vijand*—for 'enemy.' It might have been *Liane*.

Mulder swore. Visser's grip slipped.

"Do not let go," Van Helsing ordered, and drove the trocar the last inch home.

Whatever had been in the lungs left with a long, shuddering discharge. The warmth under his hands cooled by the width of a hair.

He withdrew the steel and set it aside.

"In some countries," he said, "they would stop there. Thankfully, at least for today, we live in a more thorough jurisdiction."

He picked up the saw.

Mulder closed his eyes. Visser began praying softly.

The sound of the saw on bone was the same as it had ever been: harsh, mechanical, indifferent. If there was an echo in the house of Willem De Groot, it had been driven out with the breath.

When it was done, and the head lay wrapped in its own parcel of linen, the room changed at last. A faint, sour tang crept into the air: the first hint of decay. The temperature managed to bite through Van Helsing's coat.

The next fly that wandered in from the corridor landed on De Groot's exposed wrist without hesitation.

"Help me with him," Van Helsing said.

Between them, they bore the body to a small brick furnace at the back of the mortuary, where they usually disposed of amputated limbs and pathological specimens. It had never taken a whole man before.

Mulder stoked the coals until they glowed white. Visser opened the iron mouth, and the heat slammed into Van Helsing's face.

"Professor," Visser said hoarsely, "should we say something?"

"You prayed already," Van Helsing said.

They slid the body in. The linen caught quickly. For a moment, the shape of a man remained, outlined in the fire; then it blurred, folded, and collapsed like a house of cards.

"Dear God," Mulder said, breathing hard. "How do I explain *that* in my official ledger?"

Van Helsing wiped his hands clean and reached for his notebook.

"You will say," he replied, "that under the authority of the court, the body was subjected to sanitary measures deemed necessary for the protection of the living, namely separation of the head from the neck followed by cremation. You will add that no further movement was observed."

"And nothing more?" Mulder said.

"That," Van Helsing said, "is more than enough."

He glanced once more around the mortuary: at the empty slab, at the dead fly, at the key inside the door.

"For the avoidance of doubt," he said, not without relief, "he is now entirely dead."

Outside the court, in the gray light of late afternoon, Liane De Groot stopped Van Helsing on the steps.

"Professor," she said. "A moment, please."

She seemed smaller out in the open air.

"I am in your debt," she said. "They say if you had not..." She faltered. "If you had not written it as you did—"

"I did nothing but describe what I saw," he said. "Thank the magistrate."

"I have," she said. "He told me to pray for you."

"That," Van Helsing said, "is most efficient."

She hesitated.

"What did you do to my husband, in there?"

"Exactly what the court ordered," he said. "No more, and no less."

She looked past him. For a moment, he thought she would ask the question again. Instead she pressed her handkerchief to her eyes and went down the steps alone into the November rain.

That night, in his study, Van Helsing laid out the De Groot papers across his desk. On the left, the official inquest file: the clerk's transcript of witness statements; the magistrate's summation; the jury's verdict; his own medico-legal report, with a few phrases softened for public consumption. On the right, his notebook, open at the pages Visser would never see. Between them he placed the original sanitary order in his own hand, with the magistrate's signature and seal at the bottom.

He read the report aloud, once, as if it belonged to a stranger. The curious might note the hedged references to "movement post-mortem" and "sanitary precaution"; only the very curious would wonder what exactly ended up in the furnace.

In his notebook, the same events were recorded differently.

He looked at me, he had written, in an untidy line. *The breath was warm. The eyes were too clear. The fly would not land. The second death was easier than the first.*

He closed the notebook.

On a fresh sheet, he wrote in a spare, careful hand:

Private memorandum and supplemental observations relating to the matter of Willem De Groot, to be produced only in the event that similar phenomena should recur. He signed it, as he did all his more serious work: *Abraham Van Helsing, M.D., D.Ph., D.Litt., etc., etc.*

He stacked the official file, the sanitary order, and his private notes together and bound them with red twine.

There was a space in his cabinet, behind a row of more innocent cases—typhus, an industrial accident, and the like. He slid the bundle into it, spine inward. From the corridor outside his study, no one would ever see the title.

Somewhere in Amsterdam, a clerk would be able to say that, on a certain November day, a man had his head removed from his body and was burned under proper authority, and no scandal had followed.

"As a lawyer," he said quietly, "one learns to write new forms."

He shut the cabinet.

Years later, in another country, when a different group of anxious men asked him what right he had to speak so confidently of the undead, he would think of the De Groot bundle. He would touch the papers in his coat and say, almost lightly:

"You forget that I am a lawyer as well as a doctor. There may be papers more—such as this."

For now, there were only quiet shelves, rain against the window, and the knowledge that, for one more night, the dead of Amsterdam were properly dead.

Brandon Keaton is the author of *Transference*, a quasi-religious sci-fi novel that Hugo and Nebula Award-winning author Robert J. Sawyer praised as "a crackerjack debut!" Most recently, "N-spired Learning," his short story about a sentient calculator, rather improbably won the 2025 Sir Julius Vogel Award. He is fond of comic books and gummy bears, and lives in New Zealand.

A Long Night in Wisburg
By Caolán Mac an Aircinn

*The following is extracted from the journal of
John Seward, medical student.
The beginning is lost.*

14 November, 1888.—…"On the contrary, Herr Blücher,"
Van Helsing said with a broad, toothy smile. "It is quite natural
that two men such as my student here and I should wish to ac-
quire such a specimen. For we are men of medicine, you see, and
such things by their nature fascinate us. Einfach, oder?"

The Austrian across from us, Herr Blücher, was smiling too,
but his smile was more, it seemed, a symptom of an odd sort of
panic for which I could discern no obvious cause. I wished to reassure him, but as my German is limited to comprehension and
very little speech, I could but rely on my mentor, Abraham Van
Helsing. Unfortunately, my master is not one to put a man's mind
at ease even on the best of days, and this night, in the shadowed
town of Wisburg, in a corner of the German Reich I cannot seem
to pinpoint on a map, was hardly the best of days. Herr Blücher
had insisted on meeting us in a dark, cobbled alley, repulsive with
mud and puddles and alive with the scurrying of rats, over which
the teeming, high-gabled houses crowd around like so many rela-

tives peering into an open coffin. Between the sharply angled Teutonic roofs, I can barely make out the full moon and the clouds scudding across the sky. The orange gaslights of the street do not penetrate into this alley, and such light as exists is the silvery gift of the moon. Herr Blücher had backed a borrowed farmer's cart into the alley, further than it could go—much further, for he seemed anxious that the good citizens of Wisburg not see him. On the cart, of course, was a long, quite large object covered with sailcloth, which was the object of our deliberations. The situation was such that I was quite entirely a bag of nerves. Every skitter, every jitter behind every bit of decaying rubbish only made me more nervous; and Herr Blücher, who was already nervous, seemed quite on the point of passing out.

Dr. Van Helsing, MD, D.Ph., D.Litt., etc. was, however, quite unfazed.

"What shall we say then? Twenty marks for the old girl, *ja?*"

Herr Blücher licked his lips.

"I heard, Dr. Van Helsing, that you are…"

"A man of medicine," Van Helsing interrupted him. "A man of the law, also, a man of science, a man of philosophy, and one for whom the discipline of metaphysics holds a keen interest… but no more. My interests, it is true, are wide and varied, and this fact has caused rumours to swirl about me. Discount them."

Herr Blücher licked his lips nervously again. He looked as if he were going to say something else. But the twenty Reichsmarks appeared in Van Helsing's hand as if by magic. With an odd sound, between a squeak and a strangled scream, the Austrian ripped the money from Van Helsing's hand.

"Drop the cart and horse back to Herr Stoltzmeyer's farm tomorrow morning," Blücher said. "I pray you, do not tell him what was in it. *Grüß Gott, meine Herren.*"

The Austrian was already stalking stiffly off into the night. Van Helsing ignored him, instead mounted the cart and whipped back the sailcloth.

"There we are, John," he said. "Isn't she magnificent?"

On Herr Stoltzmeyer's borrowed cart, under the sailcloth, rested a gold-trimmed wooden Egyptian coffin. Rows of hieroglyphs, fish, fowl and geometries inscrutable to all but the most bookish docent, ringed it about, as if a fence holding in its contents. The face of its inhabitant, carved onto the lid, smiled blankly up at the tortured sky; but behind her mysterious gaze lay forty centuries. I confess I have never seen anything so eerie in my life.

15 November, 1888.—I must find a less laborious way of keeping notes, for though I wish to record my ruminations, I am not in such a mood as to write them. Perhaps when I return to England I shall purchase one of Mr. Edison's phonographs. We shall see.

I am in no mood to write for I have—what is it the youth say—got the morbs, I believe is the phrase. I have passed a sleepless night, tossing and turning as I was assailed by terrors and phantasies. Such as I remember were of a distinctly Egyptian cast. I recall vast deserts of sand so white it might be taken for snow below a black sky unmarred by sun, moon, or stars; I recall rivers of fire and of black, oily water; I recall great pylons of red sandstone, guarded by creatures which walked on their hands and charged at me, demanding that I tell them their names—their names; I remember snuffling in the dark, creatures unseen hunting me throughout the hellscape of my dreams, and I was helpless as a babe throughout. I am a man of science and I cannot fall prey to superstition like some Transylvanian peasant, but I likewise cannot quite shake the notion that it is the sarcophagus, as yet unopened, occupying the corner of the room Prof. Van Helsing and I have rented here in Wisburg which is to blame for these night terrors. Even now, as I sit at the window, scratching out these notes, I will not allow my eye to wander over to it. I am not afraid of it. No. What should I be afraid of? The lid cracking, and a dusty hand reaching out from underneath? Red eyes in the darkness, whispers by cover of night? No, I am not scared. I am a man of science, after all.

I bloody well don't like it, though. That much is for sure.

Later.—My teacher, indefatigable as ever, had already gone and returned Herr Stoltzmeyer's cart before I had even tumbled out of bed. He returned shortly after I had written the passage above, wearing a wide, toothy, ironical smile with which he has seen fit to grace us more often of late. He immediately set to attempting to open the case with a pry bar. I am normally the most attentive of helpers in all things, so much do I respect Professor Van Helsing, but I cannot bring myself to assist with this, so great a distaste do I feel for what may be in that sarcophagus. Instead, I sit back and watch. Van Helsing is a striking fellow; square-chinned, red-haired, with a prominent nose and widely set blue eyes, which may charm or blaze according to his moods. He is not tall, but the force of his personality is such that he may dominate a room if he so chooses—or not, for he has that rarest of gifts: the knowledge of when to hold one's counsel. Add to this resoluteness, open-mindedness, the composure of a Stoic philosopher, and one of the finest minds Holland has ever produced, and one has a truly exceptional man. He is not, however, exceptionally blessed with physical strength, for after a minute or two of prying at the wretched case he sagged against a wall.

"*Gott im Himmel!* You try, *lieber* John. My atrophied muscles are no match for the dust of ages."

Something occurred to me as he said this.

"Professor Van Helsing, if you are Dutch, why do you use so much German?"

"I hesitate to burden you with the reason," he said. "Now, *bitte*, the dust of ages, John."

Reluctantly I took the pry bar and worked away at the sarcophagus.

"Be careful now," Van Helsing said, when too vigorous an effort on my part had splintered the edge of the lid.

"What is this thing anyway?" I asked, and I daresay a frisson of sulkiness discoloured my tone. But Van Helsing answered my question as if I had asked it honestly. He said:

"This, *lieber* John, is the corpse of Meritamen, a priestess of ancient Egypt who was buried in a time when glorious Rome and Athens were yet rude collections of mud huts. I believe she was first excavated by one of Napoleon Bonaparte's savants in Egypt, yet she has bounced from dealer to antiquities dealer in Cairo until, at last, one Herr Blücher of Salzburg, wishing a token by which to remember the Nile cruise which he had taken to mark the occasion of his retirement, purchased her. He has been trying most ardently to rid himself of her ever since."

I grunted as I wriggled the pry-bar at the coffin lid. Splinters of ancient wood flew.

"Whyever was she so hard to shift?" I asked. "Surely you're not going to tell me the old girl is haunted."

Van Helsing smiled at me enigmatically, a twinkle in his eye. I dropped the pry bar.

"Professor Van Helsing," I said, "you can't be serious."

"Of course I can be serious, John," Van Helsing said, rather obtusely. "Indeed, I am being quite serious now when I say that we must open that old coffin. Keep her intact too, you brute!"

"But why, Professor?" I finally asked. "We have paid twenty marks—good money, no small sum—to a man who would clearly have taken less, and all of it for…well, a shrivelled old priestess whom not a city full of dealers could move! What on Earth do you purport to do with this bally thing?"

"It is not," Van Helsing said gravely, "a shrivelled old priestess. Not *merely*, I should say. I paid Herr Blücher twenty marks because I am a kind man, and I wish to recompense him for some of the trouble our friend Meritamen here has caused him…and because I wished him to think us two fools. But even so philanthropic a soul as I, John, would not pay twenty Reichsmarks for a mere corpse. Here. Give me."

I must have loosened the lid a great deal, for at Van Helsing's next wrench the whole lid popped off and up into the air to land on the floor of our room with a great crash. The landlady downstairs raised up a great cry in German, which Van Helsing and I ignored. Instead we peered into the freshly open sarcophagus—he with excitement, I queasily.

Poor Meritamen, as Van Helsing called her. I was right: the years had not been kind to her. The twisted rags of bandages and the faint herbal bouquet indicated that the ancients had brought their preservational sciences to bear on her, but they had met with but little success. Meritamen's bandages had been torn from her, and her thin, sad, shrivelled, tea-leaf-brown body with its face contorted into an expression which was not so much a scream as a cry of loneliness lay half exposed. Worse still, her right arm and right leg had been torn off. Her remaining arm was clutched over her chest, as if to preserve the last scrap of modesty that her robbers had left her.

"The poor creature," I said.

"*Verdammt*," Van Helsing said. "I see what the problem is."

"Problem? What problem? Van Helsing—forgive me if I am becoming exercised, but you have not answered my question—there is a woman forty centuries dead in our rented room—you paid twenty Reichsmarks for her, yet I cannot understand—for the love of God, Van Helsing, why?"

"Do you trust me, John?"

"I do, Professor. You have been my devoted friend and companion since I sucked the gangrene from your wound—even before, if I may be so bold."

He grinned his broad, toothy grin again, and I could not but note how sharp and white his teeth were, how his eyes seemed to carry a little red, as if he had looked just a little too long into the darkness.

"Then trust me now, *lieber* John, when I say we are about to do the town of Wisburg an inestimable favour. Now: do not interrupt me again. Do you see here? Here, here and here? Where the bandages are torn? It was the custom of the Egyptians to provide charms to their dead to ease their passage to the afterlife. These have been plundered by tomb robbers. Worse still, the poor *frau* has been plundered for her medicinal properties. That, I think, is what will have happened to her limbs."

"How do you know she is a *frau*? And not a *fräulein*?"

"The hieroglyphs here, *lieber* John—it is the offering formula—in the name of her husband."

"You read Egyptian?"

"A little bit, *ja*. No more than most."

"Very good," I said, rather faintly. Van Helsing must have thought me a simpleton, for I stood there unspeaking while I gathered my thoughts. Eventually, I managed to say:

"And what of it, Van Helsing?"

"What of it? What of it, he says. What of it? My boy, the denizens of Plato's cave could scarcely match your blindness. Tell me this: how did you sleep last night?"

"Terribly, if you must know. I was assailed by visions of some Nilotic Hades the whole night long. Due, no doubt, to this horrible thing."

"*Precisely!*" Van Helsing cried. "John, three things were required for an Egyptian to make it to the afterlife: the right spells, the right charms and wholeness of body. It is these three things which are lacking for Meritamen. And so she takes her revenge with visions of doom—for now; most recently on you, and on Herr Blücher, but soon, if she is not stopped, on the whole of Wisburg. If she is not stopped soon, her depredations may take on a more material nature. It is no exaggeration to say, *lieber* John, that the dead may soon walk Wisburg if we do nothing."

"Van Helsing," I said, "I feel it is contingent on me to ask. How do you know all these things?"

"One picks them up, *ja?*" the Dutchman said happily. "If I can be a doctor and a lawyer both, it can be no object of surprise to you that I amuse myself in spare moments with the glories of forgotten Egypt. Now, John, what do you think our next step should be?"

"Burn the wretched thing, if she's causing so much trouble."

"*Ja,* could work, could work," Van Helsing said. "But it is harsh on poor Meritamen, is it not? After all, she has done no wrong. She was merely a priestess of Hathor in life, and in death an unfortunate, divested of her charms and her limbs and sold to Blücher as a tourist's trifle. She is merely lashing out, as it were, denied access to her afterlife."

"A doctor's responsibility is to the living, Professor, is it not?"

Van Helsing flashed that irritating, toothy smile again.

"A doctor's responsibility is to all mankind, even at the blurred edges."

"Well then tell me, Professor, what on Earth do we do?"

Van Helsing smiled his broad grin.

"We must provide her with what she needs to pass to the other side," he said. "You will be delighted to know that I have in that satchel over there Herr Birch's photographic edition of the Papyrus of Nebseny, which represents a manifestation of the *Todtenbuch*—excuse me, the Book of the Dead. That, John, will give her her spells. I am going to talk to some antiquarians of my acquaintance here in Wisburg. I expect they will be able to procure some scarabs for me."

"But what about her limbs?" I protested. "You can't grow those back, Professor."

He looked at me and grinned even more widely.

"Oh, no," I said. "Please, Van Helsing, I beg of you."

"For the people of Wisburg, Seward!"

"But what about *me*?"

Later.—I ought to have known better than to argue. Van Helsing always gets his way; he has a way of grinding one down. Still, I had thought that in this more enlightened age of our Queen Victoria that I could get away with being a doctor without indulging in bodysnatching. How naive I was!

Wisburg is a town periodically affected with the plague, and so my first thought was to burgle the pauper's grave in the Protestant cemetery and thence procure an arm and a leg with which poor Meritamen might be made whole once more. However, something of old Van Helsing's soft-heartedness must be rubbing off on me, for I found that I could not bring myself to desecrate the grave of so many who had done no wrong. Fortune smiled, however, for I learned from the evening paper that a notorious plagiarist in the town had been put to rest scarce three days hence. As soon as night fell, I took a shovel which Herr Stoltzmeyer had loaned Van Helsing and betook myself across town to the graveyard. For assistance, I brought a new friend I had made, a well-travelled American—a Texan, most properly— by the name of Quincey P. Morris who happens to be making his way through Germany. His accent notwithstanding, he is a splendid fellow. He says he is thinking of coming to England to find himself an English wife; I do hope we meet again there.

I confess that my thoughts took a bitter turn as Quincey and I peeled away the loam, thinking of Van Helsing smoking his pipe and drinking brandy with the idle rich of Wisburg, gleaning Egyptian antiquities from them, whereas I was condemned to slave away digging. I consoled myself that the age of widespread bodysnatching was over, and the watchtowers and mortsafes which once would have made a job such as this difficult were now nowhere in evidence. Nor could I possibly have slept in that room, with that desiccated prune of a Meritamen watching malevolently over me. Even as I left, I could hear the landlady and her other lodgers turning fitfully in their sleep, tormented with their own visions of white sands and chasing demons. Our trousers were filthy and our spats quite ruined by the time we made it to the old plagiarist's coffin. I had a thought to smash it in, but instead, out of respect, I simply opened it, made the requisite incisions with my shovel, and hurled the required limbs up to the edge of the pit. Quincey, bless him, took this all in stride, and left sharpish as soon as I paid him the ten marks I had promised. For my part, I wondered if it would make any difference that Meritamen was about to be given a man's arm and a leg. I was hauling myself out of the pit when suddenly a bright light was shone in my face.

"*Wer ist da?*"

I was confronted, beyond the blinding beam of a lantern, with the white-bewhiskered face of a blue-uniformed night watchman. What would Van Helsing do? Think of some terribly clever way out of the situation, no doubt. For my part, I jumped up out of the pit and put on my most fearsome face, and then, using my extremely weak German, I called:

"*Ich bin ein Gespenst!* I am a ghost!"

It was manifest from his raised eyebrows that the watchman did not take me for any sort of ghost. I am sorry to say it behove me to find a blunter solution, by which I mean the forceful application of the flat of the shovel to the poor watchman's forehead. He will be all right in the morning bar a fine blue bruise, for I carried him to shelter and checked to see that he was alright; but it was all the same not in keeping with the Hippocratic oath to overpower a public servant with a shovel. May God forgive me.

Van Helsing was waiting for me at the street entrance to our lodgings.

"*Gott im Himmel,* what kept you?" he hissed. I was about to deliver a tirade when he shushed me.

"Listen, John!"

He pointed to the window of our room. I did hear it then: the creaking of floorboards.

"Robbers?" I asked urgently. But he shook his head.

"Come, John," he said. "We have not much time."

I should much rather have been on the next boat to England. Why, I would sooner have gone to stay in a crumbling Wallachian castle than back into those lodgings. But Van Helsing, as I say, is not to be denied. We ghosted up the stairs, past the moans and groans of our dream-tortured housemates; and Van Helsing pushed open the door.

I had expected a scene of utmost horror, and in a manner, the sight of that shambling creature, burst forth from her case, feeling her way along the walls with the withered fingers of her remaining hand, groaning piteously, was horror at its purest; but something about the risen Meritamen seemed so helpless, so forlorn that I could not but pity her. But she was possessed of no such compunction, for no sooner did the light of Van Helsing's lantern fall upon her than she turned with shocking speed and snarled at him. Her progress on one foot was irregular, but her strength must have been immense for she charged across the room, balancing herself on what pieces of furniture there were, and grabbed Van Helsing by the neck. Him she hoisted up into the air till his face turned purple.

"*Verdammte Scheiße!*" he managed. "Seward…give her…"

"Are you out of your mind?" I shouted. "She'll kill us!"

"…give her…the damnable…"

I crossed the room, to the risen mummy, and proffered her the limbs. When she did not notice them, I made as if to fit them to her. At this she did take notice, grabbing first the putrid plagiarist's leg and balancing herself upon it as squarely as she could, then taking the arm and working it to her shoulder. Van Helsing collapsed in a shuddering heap against the wall.

"The…Birch…"

"What?"

"*Dummkopf!* The Book of the Dead!"

I remembered Van Helsing's satchel, took out the photographic copy of the papyrus, flipped it open, and laid it in her coffin. She stopped fiddling with her new arm to peer at it. At this, Van Helsing seemed to regain some strength, for he got up and hobbled across the room to the coffin, into which he placed three blue faience scarabs which he produced from inside his overcoat.

At this, the revenant, which a few seconds hence had been the very embodiment of malevolence, became docile as a lamb. Her face wore no expression, ossified as it was with age, but she shambled across the room, hauling her new limbs with her, and got back into her coffin. One hand snaked out, lifted the lid— that massive, heavy lid—one-handed, and replaced it atop the coffin with a muffled *click*. All at once, the groaning and moaning of the nightmare-sufferers about us ceased, as if turned off with a switch.

"I'll be damned," I said. Van Helsing rubbed his throat.

"It's not always about a stake through the heart," he said. "Don't mistake me, Seward: sometimes it is. But the undead are ultimately human, in their origin if not in their substance, and sometimes they can be reasoned with."

"Quite," I said. "I don't suppose you thought to bring any brandy home with you? It's been a long night."

Caolán Mac an Aircinn is a translator, classicist, and musician from Dublin, Ireland who writes both in English and in his native Irish. When he is not writing or working, he enjoys playing the Irish fiddle and bothering his cats.

Abraham
Versus the Abhartach

By Ryan Charles Lieb

LETTER, ABRAHAM VAN HELSING TO JOHN SEWARD

17 December 1898

John, my good friend—

I hope this letter, and its successors, which should be arriving in the following days, find you in the greatest possible health, as the matter about which I am writing will demand mental fortitude. You may be curious as to why I have chosen to write a series of letters instead of a single complete account of these events. The time I have to write is limited and the task ahead is perilous, therefore it is absolutely imperative that I deliver each piece of my story to you immediately, before I lose either the mental or physical capability of doing so.

I speak now of that great and terrible ordeal in Transylvania, our battle with the vampire, Count Dracula, whom we were only able to overcome with the tremendous power of our friendship. I call upon the aid of your friendship once more, though this time only in spirit, as merely writing to you gives my heart warmth and makes me feel steeled for the task ahead. Before I speak on that task, I must first apprise you of the history behind it.

It is no great confession that Transylvania was not my first encounter with the vampire. Alas, I have long been loath to speak of the events that provided me the tools and knowledge to do battle with the Count last year, as it is a matter that fills me with great shame. I was young, skeptical, not ready to believe in the existence of pure evil. In the early days of my education, I was interested in the occult, but from a purely psychological position. I endeavored to discover what drove human beings to believe in fantastic and irrational things. In my hubris, I made a pilgrimage to a place that was said to be the home of a monster. A monster which I believed must only exist inside the tenuous fabric of the villagers' uneducated minds, but was in fact, a true monster in the flesh.

This pilgrimage was a startling revelation, the event that utterly reframed my perception of reality and unblocked my mind from the tremendous possibilities of our inexplicable existence. It was also my greatest failure, which has haunted me perpetually since the day I fled.

Alas, I must conclude this preamble as my boat is nearly ready to depart. I am bound for Belfast, Ireland, where I intend to draft my second letter before departing for my final destination.

Your old and true friend,
Abraham Van Helsing

Letter, Abraham Van Helsing to John Seward

18 December 1898

John—

I have arrived safely in Belfast and am taking a short rest before boarding a carriage to Maghera, Ireland.

Let me speak to you now of the origin of the creature that I am hunting. When this tale was first recounted to me by the townsfolk of Maghera, I met it with great incredulity, feigning academic interest while scoffing internally all the while. Today, I know with absolute conviction that every word of it is true, and I suspect you should have no reservations about believing in it either, given our recent ordeals.

He is called "Abhartach." This is not a true name, but an epithet, which approximately translates to "clever one." So far as I can surmise, there are two distinct pronunciations for it. The younger villagers say "Uh-Var-Tack," with emphasis placed on the center vowel. A few of the village elders who still speak Irish Gaelic tend to soften the consonants, which sounds like "Our-Tah," when they aren't reluctant to speak the word at all. I prefer the former, as the latter sounds otherworldly to my Germanic ears and fills my heart with dread.

In the local legend, he is said to have been a chieftain, many centuries ago, when the land was wild and populated by primitive tribes. No one knows his true name, and he was said to practice dark arts. His presence caused mothers to miscarry, his breath carried a blight that made crops turn to rot, and his stare impelled the bravest of warriors to weep from fear. Death and misery followed the Abhartach's tribe. A few followers with sinister hearts gave him their loyalty and reaped the spoils of their conquests, but the great majority of his people rejected his rule and allied with a neighboring tribe to overthrow him. After a lengthy battle that cost many lives, he was finally struck down by the neighbor tribe's chieftain, and buried standing upright, as was the custom for chieftains at this time.

Of course, you can surmise that this was not the end of the story. The following month was a time of healing and convivial bonding for the two tribes. Crops flourished, healthy babies were born from joyous mothers, great feasts were had in celebration of the era of prosperity to come. Then one night, a scream echoed through the village. A tribesman had been found viciously murdered. All of his limbs had been broken, his throat had been slashed open, and his body utterly drained of its lifeblood. Most confounding of all, the blood was not soaking the ground around the body as one would expect, but simply gone altogether. And it's said that his eyes were wide and his mouth agape in an expression of unimaginable horror. Each night thenceforth, another body was found in the same manner, each tribesmen lured into the woods just outside the perimeter of the village by some un-known assailant and then eviscerated. It was a great mystery that placed the two tribes again in a state of continuous terror.

This went on for several weeks, until the culprit revealed it-self by attacking the new chieftain. It was the Abhartach, the clever one, returned from the grave to take revenge and reclaim its rule over the tribe. Its opponent, however, was a man of re-markable courage and ability, and having already slain the Abhar-tach once, did not waiver in his resolve. He bested the creature again in singular combat, driving his sword through its tainted heart, and returned it to its solitary grave.

But still, this was not the end.

Another month of merriment passed, and the cycle began again. It seemed the clever one simply would not remain dead. The chieftain, in desperation, consulted with a Druid priestess, who advised him that the Abhartach had become one of the walking dead, which can only be subdued by driving a sword made of yew wood through its heart. Having acquired such a weapon, he slew the creature one final time, and buried the Ab-hartach upside down, in defiance of the tradition of burying chieftains in an upright standing posture, thus stripping it utterly of its claim over the tribe. Finally, the Druidess advised him to place a large boulder over the grave, to ensure it would never again be able to climb out. And there the creature remained for many centuries. That is, until shortly before my arrival in Maghera.

I must again conclude my writing for today, for my carriage to Maghera has arrived. Be well my dear friend, and watch for my next letter in two days' time.

Abraham Van Helsing

Letter, Abraham Van Helsing to John Seward

20 December 1898

My old friend—

I have arrived in Maghera, this dreadful place, and already I can feel the clever one's presence. There is a terrible chill in the air, and my hand is trembling as I write, so please accept my apology if this letter approaches the limit of legibility. I can feel the Abhartach intruding on my thoughts, suggesting that I should climb the tallest watchtower and jump off, or drink the entire vial of laudanum in my emergency kit, a tempting escape from the grave matters ahead. But understand my good friend, that it will take far more than mere suggestion to undo Abraham Van Helsing's resolve.

I am currently set up in a local tavern waiting for the chief constable to arrive and discuss with him a most perilous undertaking. But before I impart the details of my upcoming plans to you, I must explain what happened during my first pilgrimage to Maghera, my original encounter with the clever one.

When I arrived here all those years ago, young and full of naivety, I met with some locals, who imparted to me the legend of the Abhartach, which I transcribed to you in my previous letter. They then showed me its supposed grave, where indeed a great boulder had once been resting but was now toppled to the side, revealing a deep crater. Had a body actually resided there and been exhumed? Or had someone dug the hole as a prank? It was a mystery, but I certainly did not believe one of the walking dead had exhumed itself from it.

More concerning to me was the fact that murders were taking place in Maghera. Just as described in the Abhartach legend, unfortunate locals were found in the surrounding woods mangled and fully drained of their blood. I concluded immediately that the culprit was some kind of copycat, someone with a deranged mind who dug the hole and committed the murders in the manner of the legend to frighten the villagers into believing the Abhartach had risen, but in fact he was only a sick person who ought to be locked in your sanitarium, or put out of his misery.

I consulted with the constabulary, thinking that with my then rudimentary understanding of psychology, I could act as an advisor of sorts, and help anticipate the killer's next move.

I was permitted to examine the most recent victim, and must confess it tested the limits of my constitution. The poor wretch's limbs had been mangled beyond hope of repair, and his throat had been torn open, exposing the larynx. The sight nearly made me regurgitate that morning's black pudding. Unlike Count Dracula, whose attacks left only a pair of small puncture wounds, these attacks were savage and uninhibited. This creature did not appear to have any desire to sire offspring, as the count did with dear Miss Lucy. None who were attacked by it were left alive to slowly turn undead, it seemed interested only in draining them utterly of life. And in that aim, it was expertly skilled, as despite the brutality of these attacks, still not a drop of blood was left behind for us to find.

After composing myself and swallowing my breakfast back down, I offered what conclusions I could. The assailant, I surmised, had to be a large, able-bodied male, and must be using some sort of large blunt weapon to destroy the limbs, like a club or a hammer. And the lack of blood indicated that the victims had been murdered at another location, where they were drained and then dumped at the crime scenes. As for the motive? I concluded that the staging of the victims as vampire attacks suggested an infantile obsession with fantasy, as only children truly believed in monsters.

Pure folly, of course, all of it. And it wasn't long before I learned just how benighted my analysis truly was. For in addition to the manhunt, we instituted nightly patrols, which I was allowed to accompany. It was on one such patrol that I came face to face with true evil for the first time. I had been walking the woods with a young and stalwart patrolman named Thomas for nigh on four hours, our torches burning low, and we were just about to turn in when we heard a scream of purest agony. We rushed in the direction of the sound, and there was the vampire, hunched over the body of the man whose voice had called us there, his mouth clamped onto the poor man's throat. The man's jaw was open wide, but he screamed no more, his vocal cords now phonating directly into the vampire's maw. But he also screamed with his eyes, which were bloodshot and attempting to turn fully inside his skull, to look at anything besides the horrible creature that was currently sucking his life away.

"Stop, you devil!" I called.

The Abhartach, startled, released its victim and turned to us with an ear-piercing shriek. Its body was covered from head to toe with dirt, and what flesh we could see was decaying, with bone and sinew exposed. Its eye sockets were sunken and the eyes themselves nothing but tiny red dots, reflecting the dying fire from our torches. It was bald and its skin was thin and translucent. But its teeth, my God John, its teeth were wholly intact and healthy, drenched in bright red blood, but underneath the blood they appeared to be pearly white and strong as steel. It had two particularly long fangs like Dracula, but all of its smaller teeth were pointed as well, and its jaw opened far wider than it should have been able to, as if the joints attaching it to the skull were missing and its decrepit cheeks could stretch to any size. When it unfurled itself from its victim it stood nearly seven feet tall, and then it rushed toward us with inhuman speed, claws outstretched. For a brief moment, I believed this was the end of my life, and I take no shame in admitting that I merely closed my eyes and accepted my fate. But my companion, Thomas, who was a practicing catholic, instinctively reached for the crucifix he wore around his neck, and held it out toward the Abhartach.

"Begone, ye foul thing! Back to the soil with ye!" He cried.

The Abhartach stopped short, as if he'd collided with an invisible wall, and roared at Thomas angrily, but Thomas stood firm. "Back! Back!" he repeated, and then the Abhartach turned the other way, and disappeared into the woods.

Unfortunately, we were too late to save the victim, but now we knew what we were up against: a true monster.

"Forget all of my previous conclusions!" I told the villagers the next night, in regard to my previous conclusions. "Assume the legends are true. What do we know about this creature? What are its weaknesses?" I asked. The crucifix was, of course, one advantage we had already discovered, but we needed as many as we could find.

It was then that one of the village elders came forward and provided us with another crucial weapon.

"Garlic!" they said. The Abhartach utterly detested garlic, according to some versions of the legend. This was the first I had heard of this, but as my modern education had almost wholly failed me, I chose to believe it. Now, I say that my education *almost* wholly failed me, mind you, because it did enable me to draw one conclusion of consequence.

"Vanity!" I said. "That is the Abhartach's fatal flaw!"

In the legend, his ultimate desire was to slay the new chieftain and reclaim his place as ruler of the tribe. Therefore I surmised that its desire presently was to render us helpless through fear, and then assume control over the village of Magerha, and possibly to expand its territory further after that. And so in order to defeat it, we would let it believe it had already won!

We erected a dais inside the townhall and placed upon it the most garish chair we could find. We instituted a strict curfew and made preparations over the course of three nights. On the fourth night, the leaders of the community and I assembled there and divided into two groups, leaving an aisle between the entrance and the dais, and got down on our knees. Once we were all in place, Thomas went to the open door and called out into the dark.

"Abhartach! Clever One! We submit ourselves to your authority! Come forth, and take your rightful place as our chieftain!"

For several agonizing moments, it seemed as if the call had gone unheeded, and I feared that the Sun would again rise on a Maghera still plagued by a devil. But then, just as I was about to call off the scheme, The Abhartach arrived. It said nothing, just shuffled in slowly, past Thomas and down the center aisle of the townhall, toward the throne we had erected. We kept our heads bowed in supplication, so initially I only saw it from the waist down. It had procured a crimson robe from somewhere, which dragged across the floor behind it, turning its muddy footprints into a long continuous streak of putrescence. It approached the throne, turned slowly to face its congregation, and took a seat. It was, as I had predicted, too enraptured by our apparent submission to sense the trap we had laid for it.

"Now!" I cried.

Someone pulled a hidden rope, releasing the many pounds of garlic bulbs we had fastened to the ceiling with a net. They were connected by circles of string, such that several of them landed around the vampire's neck and draped over its torso.

The Abhartach shrieked, its wide mouth filling the hall with sound that threatened to rupture our ear drums. It clawed at itself in a panic, attempting to rip the garlic away, but the bulbs seemed to sting its fingers.

As we had planned, each of us brandished the crosses we had hidden in our clothes, and we advanced on the vampire. Unfortunately, the first two townsfolk to confront it head on were weak in their faith, despite being sturdy in their courage. The Abhartach sent the first cross that came near it, as well as the arm that was holding it, flying across the room with a swipe of its great claw. The man whose arm it had been screamed in agony as the other claw disemboweled him. The woman who came up next lost her head in a flash. The Abhartach grabbed her torso and closed its mouth around her neck stump to get the blood gushing from it, before tossing the body aside like a rag doll.

Then Thomas, who was stronger in his faith than any man I have yet met, was upon the creature. Where the others were like flies to the vampire, Thomas was like a lion bearing down on it. The creature raised its claws as if to shield its eyes from some blinding light, and shrank away in fear. I was frozen to the spot, both in terror of the Abhartach and in awe of Thomas, until Thomas called to me.

"Now, Abraham! The stake!"

And then I recalled my part in the scheme. I removed from my robes a metal hammer and the sharp yew wood stake we had fashioned, and approached the Abhartach. When it saw me coming, it twisted in its throne and attempted to shield itself with its robe.

"Face us, ye coward!" Thomas said. The Abhartach turned to answer his taunt with a defiant screech, leaving itself open to my attack.

I plunged the stake into its chest, into the very same hole left by the stake that had subdued it all those centuries ago, which was yet unhealed. Then I raised my hammer and struck the flat end of it three times, driving it the rest of the way into the Abhartach's undead heart. With a long, shuddering exhale, the vampire went limp, seemingly dead, but we knew it was not so. It was incapacitated, but would surely still rise again.

"What do we do with it?" The townsfolk asked. They were all, including Thomas, suddenly looking to me for the answer.

"Can we behead it?" I asked.

This worked on Count Dracula, but it seems that while all vampires undoubtedly share certain weaknesses, they also differ to some degree in their physical traits and bodily makeup. This vampire's spinal column had some sort of supernatural toughness to it, for no matter how sharp and heavy the blade, nor how brawny and skilled the executioner, the head simply would not leave the body.

"Can we burn it?" Someone else asked.

I cautioned against this, for we had no idea how long it would take for vampire's flesh to burn, or if it would at all, and we risked burning up the stake that was currently keeping it dormant.

After many agonizing hours of contemplation, I gave the only advice I could think of.

"Return it to the soil whence it came. Bury it upside down and cover it with the stone, just as before."

It was an incompetent solution, I knew. The stone would hold the creature for a time, but it would not be a permanent end to its reign of terror. Someday, maybe a century from now, maybe a millennia, the stake in its heart would decompose and it would find the strength to dig itself out from under the stone once again. The townsfolk in this era would be safe, but their descendants would be destined to do battle with the vampire again, likely losing some of their lives in the process. In addition, the mere presence of the creature, even dormant, would continue to poison the minds of Maghera, causing disproportionately high levels of crime and conflict.

But I could see no other option, and so it was done, and the townsfolk thanked me. Thomas even gifted me one of his crucifixes as a keepsake, which I have kept to this day and used in the battle against Count Dracula. But I could not, and still cannot, absolve myself of the feeling that I have failed them. I departed in shame.

And now that I have come to the end of my great failure, I must cease my writing, as I am presently late for a meeting with Thomas. He is now the Chief Constable here, and we are to discuss a plan to correct my failure. Given the complexity of the tasks at hand, I am not certain when I will have time to write again, therefore my next letter may not arrive for several days.

Worry not, and be well, my good friend.

A. Van Helsing

Letter, Abraham Van Helsing to John Seward

25 December 1898

John—

Have you figured it out, my friend? The secret of the Abhartach's resurrection, why it was able to dig itself out of its grave that was meant to hold it for eternity? I suspect you put your finger on it a week ago, and can imagine you screaming at my letters as you read them, cursing my ignorance.

"Abraham! You imbecile! It's the soil! The *soil!*" You might be saying.

And yes, I believe you are correct!

As we learned in our battle with Count Dracula, the soil of a vampire's homeland has a life preserving effect on its body. And so, to truly destroy the Abhartach, it should not have been buried in Maghera, but in a land where the soil does not connect with that of Ireland at all, a land separated by a vast ocean. Theoretically, London should be a sufficient distance, but out of an abundance of caution, I have decided to take him even further, to my home city of Amsterdam, where I am currently bound by boat.

Yesterday, I regaled Thomas with the story of our battle with Dracula, so that he would understand and agree with my conclusion that the soil is the key. We then filled a coffin with Maghera soil, exhumed the body of the Abhartach, and interred it in the coffin. We feared all the while that it would snap awake and rip our throats out, but it remained stiff and lifeless, the stake still firmly in place. And yet, I could sense its awareness, and its malice. Despite being immobile, it is still very much alive and wants me dead more than anyone.

We transported it by caravan to Belfast, where we boarded the ship from which I am now writing. I paid the captain a handsome sum to circumvent the island of England and head nonstop to Amsterdam. Already the journey has been perilous. A murder occurred not an hour from departure. The culprit was found and claimed that voices compelled him to the deed. All of the non-essential passengers, including myself, have been confined to our quarters for fear that we might further harm each other, or hurl ourselves into the ocean, which I admit is something I desperately desire to do. I have left Thomas in charge of the ship as he is both steadfast in his faith and a skilled leader, and I have entrusted my emergency medical kit to him so as to keep it out of my possession. There are far too many chemicals and instruments contained therein that I could use to kill or disfigure myself. As far as I am aware, the creature still has not risen from its crate as we all feared it might, though under present conditions I wouldn't know if it has until it breaks down my door and rips my throat out. We have a Catholic priest blessing the coffin with holy water every hour, though whether he is still alive I cannot be sure. Regardless of its physical state, the Abhartach's power over our subconscious minds is immense, and I only hope the wind is at our backs so that this mission can be completed before this ship goes the way of the Demeter.

This will be my final letter. If you find it unconcluded, it will mean that I am dead, and this letter was found in the wreckage. It will also mean that a vampire is loose somewhere in Amsterdam.

If, however, we reach Amsterdam and are able to safely finish our business with the Abhartach, then I will conclude my story on the backside of this parchment. For now, I must attempt to get some sleep and silence my untrustworthy thoughts. Be well my friend.

(written on the letter's backside)

How relieved are you, my friend, to find that this side of the parchment is not blank?

Yes, I have made it to Amsterdam, and The Abhartach is returned to the ground! Raise a drink with me, for I suspect the reading of these letters has been nearly as taxing for you as dealing with the Abhartach has been for me.

Two more poor souls tragically succumbed to the vampire's mental poison and jumped into the ocean while I was interned in my cabin, but besides that, Thomas performed admirably in keeping the ship on its course, the priest maintained his wits and did not abandon his duty to keep the coffin blessed, and the vampire did not so much as stir for the entirety of the trip.

Unwilling to inter the creature in the city near such a large, unwitting population, we brought it to my own estate and dug a hole near the outskirts of the property. We hired two gravediggers and paid them generously for their silence, and commissioned them to take the coffin and dump the Irish soil into the ocean. We buried the Abhartach upside down just as in the legend, and even found a stone to cover it with, though it is my sincere belief that all of this was unnecessary. From the moment we placed the last shovel full of dirt and packed it down, I felt a great weight lift from my heart. The soil of the Netherlands has silenced the Abhartach's mental powers, and somehow I know that it is already consuming its body too. In fifteen years or so, should I decide to exhume this grave, I expect I will find only bones, and then I will feel truly absolved.

Thank you, my friend, for though you were but a passive observer in this tale, merely thinking of your friendship gave me the strength to return to Maghera, and knowing you were waiting in suspense for the conclusion of my story gave me the resolve to see it through to the end.

And now I must turn in for what I expect will be the greatest sleep I've had since my first pilgrimage to Maghera, all those decades ago.

Be well, my good friend, and Merry Christmas!
Your eternal friend,
Abraham Van Helsing

Ryan Charlies Lieb is a musician and horror writer from Omaha, NE. This short story combines his love of gothic literature, horrifying vampires, and Irish folklore. His short story "Fatal Gaze" was previously featured on the Creepy Podcast.

Voileta's Life of Grim Purpose
By David Rider

When he introduced himself as Abraham she stated that names between strangers are best saved for goodbyes.

He countered with, "But this will be a long carriage ride, madame. What shall I call you until our farewell?"

"How old are you?"

"Thirty."

"I'm three years older. Do I look like a 'madame' to you?"

"Forgive me. I saw your ring and assumed."

Too late, she covered her left hand with the other. All the digits on her right hand had rings. This made the single diamond ring on her left stand out. "Assumptions about me are wasted."

"Yet I can safely assume your nationality."

Her green eyes were piercing. "Eh? You would continue?"

"If you allow it."

She opened her arms, inviting appraisal. "Astound me."

He leaned forward from his seat opposite hers. "Disregarding features, I can tell from clothing alone."

Their fellow passenger, a banker, peered over his copy of the *Liverpool Mercury* as if wanting in on the game. His private guess, based on her appearance, was Italian.

"I am a seasoned traveler, miss. I have seen dresses with patterns similar to yours in Hungary. I have seen the bows in your braids worn by Moldavian women. However, your purple shawl and its fringe looks to be your most weathered accessory. I have seen its like in a Bucharest marketplace. Given your varied fashion sense, I believe you to be Romani."

The banker scowled with disdain, returning to his newspaper.

Other than crossing her arms, she didn't react.

"Am I correct?"

She leaned forward. "Now let me guess what you are."

He chuckled. "You wish to start a new game without concluding the first?"

"I do. Mine will be quick. You're Dutch."

"I am."

"You're also a soft school boy."

He blinked at her tone.

"When you're not traveling, you attend university. How you afford either activity is unknown. Your clothing is cheap. You don't come from money."

"Orphaned at birth. I endured."

"Your cricketing bag has college tags, but is likely full of books. I doubt you play sports. You have the frame for rugby but your hands are like an infant's. You may hold a degree or two."

"Three. Working on a fourth."

"Yet master of none, eh? You've little life experience outside your hallowed halls of learning. I'll bet you travel from place to place exploring libraries. Reading tomes in languages you don't speak."

"I speak five. Working on a sixth."

"You've no sense of purpose, have you?"

It was his turn to cross his arms.

"So, Abraham the Orphaned School Boy, what *is* your purpose in life?"

He grumbled something under his breath about how he was done giving answers when she would provide none. He added, "What is yours?"

She gazed out the window. "You wouldn't believe me if I told you. I choose not to."

He still didn't know what to call her.

The carriage ride continued in silence.

Their introduction left him salty and her sullen. This would prove to be her natural state, as he came to learn after reaching their destination in Ormskirk. Abraham offered to help with her leather satchel. She refused. They emerged into a brisk September morning. Her parting words were meant to be, "The library's over there," but his reply held curiosity: "And where will you go?"

She looked up at him, a mannish boy twice her size, and made a decision in the moment. "My adventure begins here. Where it ends I hope to learn before day's end. I suspect Scotland." She shouldered her bag and turned to leave. And, as she expected, he posed a one-word question before her first step.

"Adventure?"

She glanced back over her shoulder, cocking an eyebrow. "More of a mission."

He took it for the invitation it was and went with her.

Their walk to the center of Ormskirk brought them to a bustling open market. The area smelled strongly of baked goods. They stopped at a fountain. She consulted written directions and he munched on gingerbread purchased from a vendor. He peered over her shoulder at the neat scribblings in her notebook, but couldn't decipher the language. When asked for confirmation that she was Romani, she replied, "This way," and led him away from the market.

Upon arriving at a small home, she whispered before knocking. "They'll call me a name that's not my own. Act like it is. Say nothing else."

He shrugged. "How would I know if it is not?"

This would be the first of three residences she brought him to on their journey north. Two others were in Penrith and Carlisle. The common denominators in each were the same: a widower answered the door. All three men had lost a wife and also a son. They called her by the name Evangeline. All had corresponded with her.

In the Ormskirk home, a man shrunken with age and grief invited them inside. They were seated in a tiny living room and served tea and biscuits. As this first conversation progressed, it became clear that she was there to interview the father about his son. He explained how the boy died of disease at fifteen and had been lain to rest. Soon after, his mother began seeing his face in her window at night. It drove her mad. She took her own life.

After leaving that house, his companion said, "His son is the twelfth death I've confirmed since starting this mission." She put a check by the boy's name in her notebook.

In Penrith, they met with another hollow-eyed man. His son was the thirteenth death. His wife had also gone insane over many months. After being admitted to an asylum, she claimed her dead boy visited through the bars of her second-floor cell. One night she escaped long enough to dash to the roof and hurl herself off.

In Carlisle they spoke with a fourteenth boy's father whose story was much the same. His tormented wife told tales of witnessing their son leaving the family crypt in the company of a pale man she saw only from behind. Upon returning from a business trip, the husband found her in the garden with a broken neck.

Abraham was affected by these tragic stories, and told her so. He had great empathy for the grieving fathers. She countered with, "And what of the mothers' heartaches?"

"Them, too, obviously."

They crossed into Scotland as the sun touched the horizon. He pushed for details about her mission.

"After this next one."

They arrived in the border town of Gretna Green. There they uncovered a somewhat different account from a pair of ginger-haired parents. Their daughter had gone missing the summer before. Presenting her image on a tintype, they gave her age as seventeen. Older than any of the dead boys but looking younger, she was thick of frame, appearing masculine to Abraham's eyes. One springy copper curl hung loose over her forehead; the rest were concealed under a derby. She wore trousers and suspenders. The parents didn't explain her state of dress. That the girl looked male fit the pattern of boys being targeted.

What made this interview unique was that both parents had seen their daughter speaking with a pale man by the road before her disappearance.

Abraham's companion opened her notebook to show them a sketch. "Is this him?"

The mother covered her mouth. "Och! That's the very devil she was with the night we saw her last!"

The charcoal portrait depicted a man's gaunt face. His hair was long, dark, and stringy. His beard was patchy. The skin below his eyebrows was rendered in thick shadow; the only light in his eyes being reflected pinpricks where his pupils would be.

The father nodded. "Eyes as black as the Earl of Hell's waistcoat! But in one respect your drawing is wrong."

"How so?"

"In twilight, his eyes were lifeless. They didnae reflect our house lights. But when he saw me coming to usher my child indoors, I'll never forget what the lamplight revealed." He paused, reliving it. "His irises glowed red like an animal's."

"In the morn, our bairn was gone from her room," the mother said. "We haven't seen her since."

She stoked the flames of their roadside campfire.

Abraham held out his hands for warmth. He had wanted to find an inn, but she dismissed his suggestion as a waste of money. In truth, he was uneasy being outdoors after the day's dark tales.

"I have a better sense of your mission."

"I'd expect no less."

"'Tis a manhunt."

"Not exactly." She spat in the flames, and retrieved a copper flask from her bag. After a healthy swig, she passed it to him.

He winced at the biting aroma, asking what it was.

"*Țuică*. Traditional fermented plum spirits aged in barrels. Pilfered from an orchard on the grounds of an Orthodox monastery in Bukovina. The drink is an adventure unto itself. It'll put hair on your chest, eh?"

He waved it away. "I have enough hair."

She took another gulp, hissing through her teeth.

He moved closer to the fire. "Why the name Evangeline?"

She leaned against the felled tree trunk at her back. "Because these men might not agree to meet with someone with a Romani name, much less allow one in their home to talk about deceased family members. It's harder to turn someone away once they've been invited and appear on a doorstep. Did you fail to notice their expressions when they saw me?"

"I…did not. Why would it matter?"

She scoffed. "Do you not know history, college boy? Theirs or your own?"

He tried on an indignant expression. "Of course I do."

"Here's a special word in your language: *heidenjachten*. Translate it for me."

"It means 'heathen hunt.' Why?"

"In the Dutch republic, my people were referred to as heathens. We were slaughtered by the score. Purged to eradicate us from within your precious borders. How do you not know this?"

He had no answer.

She was flummoxed. Finding she could no longer look at him, she laid on her side and faced the flickering flames. Orange light danced in the emerald of her eyes. "I'm on a hunt of my own. But not of innocent people ordered by a government. Rather, I mean to put down a killer of boys and a tormentor of women. Not a man. Something worse." Before he could say more, she cut short his reply. "I'll tell you in the light of day. You may not sleep otherwise."

His dreams were frightful amalgams of startling images: a boy's vacant face peering in through an upper window…and a nightmare that included a memory from Abraham's past.

This memory was triggered from his intellect pushing back against the Scottish father's claim about eyes reflecting red light. As a man of science, Abraham understood that humans do not have a *tapetum lucidum* behind the retina allowing for such eyeshine. But the year previous, while traveling between semesters, he had seen the phenomenon for himself.

He was staying in a château nestled in the France countryside. After a numbingly long carriage ride, he had unpacked and gone for an evening stroll to stretch his legs. The proprietor furnished him with a kerosene lantern, cautioning that the sky was moonless and a blanket of fog had settled. "Do not wander far," the man warned. "For there are beasts in the night."

"Wolves?"

The man hesitated before nodding.

He kept his walk short, wandering no farther than the edge of the estate before turning back. This was when he saw the figures. One tall and one short. He had the impression they had followed him away from the château, and his sudden turn was unexpected. In a startled tone, he called, *"Bonne soirée,"* but his greeting was not returned. He was disturbed to find that as he approached them through the soupy fog, he was getting no closer—as if they were backing away. The gravel crunched under the soles of his shoes, but their footfalls betrayed no sound. He broke into a cold sweat.

He raised the lantern to confirm they were human. Through a brief break in the mist, he saw two sets of eyes reflected as iridescent red orbs. The taller one—the only one having any measure of detail against the château's backlit glow—was a clean-shaven male with long sideburns. He wore a top hat and waistcoat. The other stood a head shorter. Whether it was a man or woman could not be determined.

Then the proprietor appeared behind them, calling out that dinner was served. Before his lamp could reveal further details, the figures dispersed within the tendrils of fog.

The next morning Abraham journeyed to a library to research what he encountered. The term in French was nearly identical to the one in his own language.

Y ou hunt a *vampier*."

While he told her of his past encounter, she brewed morning coffee over the flames, nibbling on biscuits. He realized she must have taken food from the houses they visited when she passed him an apple from her bag.

"Do you feel fortunate?"

He frowned.

"You stared death in the face, times two, yet walked away unharmed."

"I was unaware *what* I was seeing, or what would have happened if not for the proprietor's timely intervention."

"And now that you do…?"

He failed to take her meaning.

"Knowing my mission leads us towards death, do you choose to continue?"

"I have yet to accept that *vampiers* exist. It would require you providing me with answers." He took a bite of the apple. "I will not proceed towards danger without being armed with knowledge."

She splashed a shot of *țuică* into her coffee. "Oh, I'll tell you everything you need to know. It may well scare you away from my side."

"I scare, but not easily."

She sipped her drink, eyeing him through the steam. "What if I told you at least one of us will die in the days ahead, eh?"

He pushed for explanation.

That was an additional secret she held until later.

By chance, during lunch in a Lockerbie pub, a balding patron stopped at their table. His glance had fallen upon the sketch in her notebook. "That's Gregor MacTervish. Ye're not a friend of that *lavvy heid*, are ye?"

Abraham saw her expression flicker. She had intentionally opened the book to nab the passing man's attention. That the ploy worked—and a name was dropped in her lap—surprised her. She recovered, but fumbled the name's pronunciation.

"The bastard MacTerbish *has* no friends."

"Aye!"

Abraham offered to buy the man a pint.

He downed three, and told a profanity-laden tale of a stranger who arrived in town two winters ago. This "confidence man" claimed to be the brother of Gavan MacTervish, a wealthy, reclusive baron living in a castle outside town. He fell ill soon after his long-lost brother's arrival.

"Let me guess," she said. "The baron died and Gregor became the estate's heir."

"Aye. Nary a soul in the Shire of Dumfries believe that ghastly prick to be who he claims."

Abraham met her steely gaze, asking the next question before she did. "Where is this castle?"

They erected a blind in the forest, across the road from the MacTervish grounds. Over several nights, they monitored the property using a telescope mounted on a tripod with its barrel poking through the cloth. During these nights she told Abraham what she knew of vampires and Gregor himself.

"The *mullo*, or Undead, as we call them, have existed for centuries." She explained her ancestors had encountered them in every European country through which their tribe had traveled. She had transcribed her people's oral history of the Undead into written word; logging everything from their traits to how to exterminate them. Her satchel contained notebooks filled with folklore specific to these "plague-carriers."

Abraham, who considered himself an expert on the subject of diseases, asked her to elaborate on this term.

"A *mullo* who drinks human blood can sire another of its kind by forcing their victim to drink the unholy ichor polluting their own dead veins. Now there are two. And if those two continue spreading their foul disease with abandon, and so on? It would become a pandemic."

Abraham whispered, "The Black Death in the modern world. A pestilence spread not by fleas on rodents but by monsters in human form."

Her silhouette nodded. She had forbidden campfires for fear of discovery, and was an ebony shade against the blind's wall. More chilling than the notion of a plague were her next words. "This is what MacTervish has been doing to boys from here to Liverpool. He infects them and Turns them in ways most craven. After rising from their graves, they become emotionless killers. He commands them to torment their families."

"How do you know this?"

She hesitated, intaking a breath without answering until seconds had passed. "What's important is I've identified a pattern unique to this particular spawn of the Undead. It began with his first…victim…to his second, and so on. He has followed a consistent route. The missing girl? She vanished recently. But the other boys, numbers fourteen through twelve, were taken in that order in years past, in a southerly direction."

They heard activity from the MacTervish grounds.

Abraham was closest to the telescope's eyepiece. He peered through it as she poked her head beyond the blind's edge.

A carriage pulled by black horses came up the grooved, tree-lined path. The driver wore a brimmed hat low over his eyes. As the conveyance veered onto the road, she said, "It's him! He's heading away from town."

Abraham squinted but saw only the carriage's empty interior—until he took his eye away from the telescope. Through a hole in the blind he spotted the pale man—the one from his companion's drawing—sitting inside. MacTervish's cold gaze swept the forest.

"Why could he not be seen through my telescope?"

"Are there mirrors in that thing?"

"Yes."

"The Undead cast no reflection." She watched until the carriage took a forked road south. "He hungers. I'm betting he'll travel to another village, miles away, and may not return until sunrise. We'll study his habits before taking action."

Abraham said nothing until the hoofbeats of the horses faded. "Please continue with your theory of an observed pattern."

"I believe the Undead follow a migration instinct."

"Like a bird's?"

"Similar. MacTervish journeys to Liverpool each year, as if compelled to return there. It may be the site where he was Turned. The deaths of fourteen children, plotted by day and location on a map, prove my point. He then comes back home, to the north."

"He was a Scotsman living here in the Lowlands?"

"I believe he was a Scot from elsewhere." Her voice dropped to a whisper. "If my suspicions are right, he's also the worst possible version of the Undead."

"What could be worse?"

"The monster whom we hunt going by the name MacTervish was originally the infamous murderer known as the Bloody Butcher of the Highlands."

Abraham's jaw dropped.

"You and I stalk an entity who, when alive, was a prolific killer of some two dozen innocent souls."

Tales of the Butcher's unspeakable acts were known throughout Europe. Between 1853 and 1855, a wave of terror washed over the Highlands from Oban to Inverness. Adolescent boys and young women went missing. Their bodies were found hanging by their feet, gutted like game. In the rare instances where a suspect was sighted—and one case where a would-be victim escaped his clutches—the killer's description matched his companion's sketch.

Knowing the vampire they sought was already an accomplished murderer before his transformation into an unholy killing machine fueled further nightmares. Abraham insisted on staying in an inn during the day. He slept poorly, and awoke bathed in sweat the next two afternoons.

Each time his companion remarked, "Have you decided to go back to Amsterdam?"

He glanced at her, reclining in a chair with her shoes propped against the bed, having paused her note-taking.

Both times he replied, "No."

On the last day, when asked about their evening plans, she gave an unexpected answer. "Tonight we'll invade the castle after MacTervish leaves."

"At night?! What sense does that make?"

"Do you trust me?"

"What?"

"Your *trust*. Do I have it?"

He didn't answer.

"If not, say so now, eh? I'll leave and complete my mission alone. And you can sleep knowing your adventure has ended."

He paused. "You have my trust."

"Then close your eyes. I'll tell you the rest of what you need to know tonight."

He rolled over and dreamt of bodies swaying upside-down from tree limbs.

The cold wind's whistling unnerved him. It blew through the blind's open ends. She wore the shawl over her head to warm her ears. He turned up his jacket collar and crossed his arms. She offered her flask. He refused, commenting that on previous nights MacTervish had left by now. She downed the contents and opened another flask. "Here, it warms the blood."

"I said no. I want to know your reasoning for entering the castle at night."

"Because I'll die in sunlight."

Her tone was so matter-of-fact it stunned him.

She turned her back to him and curled on the ground. "Come. Huddle next to me or we'll freeze."

He did as requested, spooning behind her small frame. He smelled the spirits on her breath when she whispered over her shoulder, "No funny business, Abraham the School Boy. Though a widow, I still consider myself married, eh?"

They stayed that way in silence for a while.

"My son was taken at the age of twelve. My husband interfered and was killed. This happened on the outskirts of Liverpool, where we had set up camp. I saw MacTervish do this. Saw his fangs. Recognized him for what he was. The constables found my boy the next day, drained and lifeless. 'Another dead Gypsy,' they said. He may not have been the first victim, but that's where my life's grim purpose began. I seek vengeance. I'm armed with weapons and the knowledge of my people to put him down. And I'll die in the process.

"I have *chovihanis* in my bloodline. Shamans, to you. Mystics gifted with the Sight. Each has foretold the same vision: my end comes in a castle, in the light of day. This is why we move at night, while the devil is gone. We'll prepare an ambush for his return. We'll move in haste. No hesitation. A hunter doesn't negotiate with their game, eh?" She pressed an elbow back into Abraham's sternum. "We'll drive iron needles and pine stakes here, piercing his heart. Decapitate him. Since the Undead can be hurt by holy objects—things blessed by priests—we'll sprinkle communion wafers over his ashes and—"

"Ye'll die, lassie, before ye see me comin'."

A voice. Outside the blind. Scarcely louder than the wind. They tensed.

Then she was yanked from Abraham's arms into the night.

"See ye in the castle, lad. Or flee and save yer hide."

An unseen blow to the skull rendered him unconscious.

Abraham awoke with a start, consciousness delivering sudden awareness of his predicament, and another distressing fact: the lightening sky heralded a coming dawn.

Hours had passed.

Was his companion dead?

This question provoked another.

Did he owe her anything?

Unexpected instinct propelled him into action. He transferred weapons from her satchel into his bag, disposing of his books in the process. All that remained were several flasks and her notebooks. He took a long sip from a flask, winced, and stuck it in a pocket. The spirits didn't calm his roiling gut.

Abraham paused long enough to open the cover of her current journal.

Property of Mrs. Voileta V.

He wrapped her journals inside the blind, and wedged the bundle between a tree's roots.

Shouldering his bag, he jogged across the road, and pushed through MacTervish's open gates.

A plan germinated and took root as he navigated the dark path through the trees. He was sprinting by the time he broke into the clearing and beheld the castle: a fifteenth century stone fortress, four stories high, with gargoyles atop the battlements. Above the arched entrance, an iron portcullis was raised, inviting him inside. He accepted, throwing open the oak doors and striding into a massive foyer.

Waiting inside was a man in black wearing a brimmed hat. Abraham recognized him as the carriage driver—who was also the pub patron that identified MacTervish in the notebook.

The driver held out his hands, saying "Stop, ye *walloper!*"

Abraham muttered, "The Undead fiend employs local spies!" and barreled through him with a lowered shoulder.

The man was launched backwards, striking his head on the marble bannister of a grand staircase. He crumpled and stayed down.

He hastened onward through a wide, opulent hall, seeking basement stairs, and found them beyond the kitchen. They led down into darkness. The air in the passage reeked of spoiled meat. The smell grew worse as he descended.

Abraham reached bottom, emerging into a rank dungeon. Torches mounted in sconces were spaced so infrequently they left shadowed voids between the gothic columns.

"This way to yer doom, boy."

He faced the direction from which the voice came, and proceeded toward a chamber where the ceiling sloped to a scant eighteen inches above his head. The buzzing of insects filled his ears. The odor was overwhelming. This was a charnel pit. Death permeated the grimy stones. His companion could not possibly still be alive in such a macabre place.

Nearing the expanse's far end, he found this assumption to be incorrect. He approached a throne flanked by standing torches. Their light revealed MacTervish sitting in wait. On the ground at his feet, the Romani woman moaned in pain. One eye was swollen shut. Her other lifted to meet Abraham's gaze. She struggled to prop herself up, and turned her head to show him her throat. Two puncture wounds were haloed by purpled skin; the rest of her complexion was pale as parchment.

"I know this lass," MacTervish said. His lips were slicked with red. Sharp fangs gleamed in a twisted grin. "It's rare when a bitch-mother comes for me."

Abraham set his bag down.

MacTervish steepled his fingers under his chin. The long nails were curved like talons. "This cur's taste is sickening. Her blood is fouled by so much drink it burns. Unlike that of her wee son."

She drew her legs under her, groaning in rage.

MacTervish's cruel smile widened. "Now *his* blood was sweet. I never forget the tasty ones. It's been years since I drank a nectar so—what're ye doin'?"

Abraham dumped the weapons from his bag onto the floor. Hatchets, blades, stakes of iron and wood, and heavy mallets clattered and echoed throughout the dungeon. "I intend to give my friend a sip of liquid courage. Then the two of us will put you down like the diseased beast you are."

"Now see here…"

Abraham retrieved the flask from his jacket and unscrewed the cap. He came toward his companion, bending to offer a drink.

She lifted a hand to accept. Her trembling fingers found the flask. Seeing he wasn't going to release it, she raised a curious eyebrow.

Abraham said, "Your trust. Do I have it?"

She gave a curt nod.

"As you advised," he whispered, "a hunter does not negotiate with game." He spun with sudden motion, shaking the flask at the seated monster.

The *țuică* splashed over MacTervish. Where it landed on the exposed skin of his raised hands the flesh peeled and smoked with startling immediacy.

Abraham anointed him again with crisscrossing motions.

The vampire shrank and writhed in his throne, acrid smoke wafting from opening wounds.

His companion summoned her strength and scrambled for a weapon. She found one and wheeled around.

MacTervish sprang forward, casting Abraham aside like he weighed eight stone less than he did—only to find his Romani victim waiting in his stead, winding back with a scythe. He managed to slash her midriff with his talons. This would be his last act before she swung her blade. His head was lopped off and spun away from the neck.

She dropped to her knees, clutching her stomach.

MacTervish's body dropped onto its back.

Abraham kicked the grisly head away, disgusted. He fumbled for the mallet and stakes, and knelt by the twitching corpse. With a grunt, he hammered the sharp pine into MacTervish's heart. The Undead body combusted and imploded into black ash.

Abraham turned to attend to his companion.

She was unable to staunch the flow of blood. Still, she smiled up at him. "How did you…?"

"Oh, the *ţuică*? I remembered you told me the plums were taken from a monastery. I once learned in a library book that priests tend to bless fruit-bearing trees."

She laid back on the ground, having enough strength to pat his cheek. "You listen well, Abraham the Orphaned School Boy. You're smart and brave. Your mother…would've been proud, eh?"

I n the end, before she bled out, Abraham carried her up a spiral staircase to the tower's roof.

He set her down against a stone alcove, positioned in full view of the sun's rays shining between parapets. They cast the shadow of a gargoyle centered atop the eastern-facing battlement, gazing out at the bright horizon.

"Here is fine," she said with a dry chuckle. "Fitting that I die facing a monster's back. The *chovihani* didn't reveal that part."

He sat and took her hand. "Did they tell you anything else?"

"Only…that I wouldn't…be alone." She squeezed his fingers with what little strength she had left. "That I would be held by a stranger…a kind and strong one."

"You always *knew* I would come."

"As long as I didn't…give my name…"

"Yet I learned it, Voileta, and I came for you anyway."

She smiled. "By the way…you never told me…"

"Told you what?"

Her eyes fluttered and closed. "Your life's purpose…?"
In truth, he hadn't known.
Not until she passed away in his arms.
Only then.

David Rider grew up roaming the alleyways of Calumet City, Illinois. Like most Gen X kids, he lived an unsupervised, feral existence of dreaming and fighting. He currently lives with his wife, kids, and dogs in a rural Midwestern town surrounded by farmland. He still daydreams, but saves the fighting for dark entities lurking within the cornfields.

He is a member of the Horror Writers Association. His stories have appeared in various anthologies from Dead Sky Publishing and Sinister Smile Press. He has published three novels, *We Are Van Helsing* Books One and Two, and *Anca's Undead Playlist*.

Ever Blooming
By Noemi Novembre

He was born late and fast to bloom. Your wife, your joy, she already had some gray streaks in her dark hair, stars among the black of her sky. You were already forty winters old, your red hair withering like a northern sunset. She sprang in your office, wild eyes and a laugh, the queen of all the laughs. She was dressed in white, like a ghost in the morning light. She said it into your ear, the news. Your students cheered in the hallway, and you cheered the more.

He was born late. You are a doctor and you knew the myriad of things that could have gone wrong; she always made everything seem so right. You knew the myriad of things that could have gone wrong, but in the midwinter you met the only right things you didn't already know: he had your wife's dark eyes and his hair was as red as yours at the dawn of your days.

You called him Isaac. He was fast to bloom like the garlic seed your wife kept by the window of her drawing room. He loved listening to her explaining folktales and myths, and roaming around while she wrote her articles for the ladies' gazette and you reviewed an essay.

He was fast to bloom, like a red lily in the snow. He had your wife's wit tongue and he had his head deep in Amsterdam's clouds, like you.

He went to Styria on a journey for his art studies.

"Just a few weeks", he said.

And you counted the days, fogged by anxiety. Just a few weeks is so much, like a myriad of things that could go wrong. But your wife had the queen of all laughs, and everything seemed too right.

He went to Styria on a journey; he came back withered, like a lily in the snow. His fever undying, his dreams too deep. What did he dream of? His bride-to-be, he dreamed of her, calling her name, and not seeing her, pale as a ghost at his bedside. Your son dreamed of drowning, drowning in his fever, while his mother watched him wither. She wept and wept, and you both, with all your knowledge, couldn't fathom an explanation. He lost blood, like a candle its light, and you didn't know why or when. He was never anaemic; it was in Styria that he caught the disease. Why? Your books don't tell, your wife's folktales could. You just give him your blood, like you did before he was born. But a tale is just a tale, and a dead man tells no tales.

He was born late, fast to bloom, and withered too soon. She laughed and laughed, your wife, the queen of all laughs, with sorrow and pain, like an animal which has lost a limb in a trap. You both did, lose a limb.

He was sharp and pale, two red dots on the neck, like in her folktales. In your nightmares he sits across the table, like he did on Sunday mornings, Andersen tales on his lap. He sits here and judges you with his mother's eyes (she never judged you, but you are your worst judge). He scrims through the pages, fingers as white as clay. His teeth as sharp as your pain. You wake up next to her, still clutching his drawing like a sleeping child clutches a ragged doll. Garlic flowers out of the window. These are only folktales, you keep saying to yourself. He died of a fever, anaemic, you keep saying to yourself.

Dots on his neck, that's a thing of folktales. Folktales like your wife always loved to tell by the fireplace. That's madness, thinking them true, and you know that. It's the sharp teeth of grief, madness lying underneath, a mirror of delusion, and you know, and you are a doctor but you can't heal yourself. That's a thing of folktales, until it's not.

Lilies sprout on the ground, like ghostly news in the newspapers. Young women with dots on their neck, a disease that's spreading. Among young women. Your son's bride-that-would-have-been, she dreams of him again and again; she wears a ribbon dark as red wine around her neck. She's happier than you've ever seen, fervent with fever. She has seen him, and you know she doesn't talk of a dream, she has seen him and you don't ask, because that's not an old man's business what young lovers do.

You gather your books and folktales. Your wife studies you, her mind is always as sharp as a mirror. You find her at your desk, wide eyes like your son, a desperate look, something is cracking but you don't know if it's her or you. She asks for an explanation, and she asks again and again. Because that's folktales, that's for the madman, and her man isn't mad. You don't know if you are mad. You don't know what's true. And you tell her just that— you don't know. Frightened like her. And your kisses wipe away her tears, and you love each other like you have since the dawn of your days.

She lies between the sheet, her hair a pool of stars and darkness. You get up in silence like a thief. She asked you, between the sleep and the wake, if he's really walking on the Earth why he didn't come home at least once. A wound deep in her voice, she didn't say "alive" or "un-dead", your son will always be what he was, and you know that and that wounds you too. If he walks on Earth, why didn't your boy come home? You know the answer even if you didn't say it, you know, while you pick the flowers out of the window and put the little bouquet at her side like an amulet. Garlic flowers.

You walk Amsterdam's foggy streets like a ghost. You don't feel alive or dead, maybe you are the real un-dead. Maybe it's just madness. Maybe you will find only worms and death, and your madness will dissolve like a cloud into the night sky.

The tomb lies between two oak trees, a weeping angel guarding it. You're weeping too, maybe it's better not to disturb his slumber. When he was a child he was afraid of the night, he would climb next to you in bed when it was stormy and you had to entertain him with stories of immortal turtles and ugly ducklings. But this night is kind, even if it's foggy. And you must know.

The grave lies open, you're still weeping like the angel, hands dirty with mud. Your boy, he lies still, like he did as a child slumbering in a dream. His hair red as the blood on his lips, a thin thread of red sealing his lips, sealing your fate. You want to close the tomb and go home, forgetting all of this, instead of doing what you have to do. A wooden stake trembles in your hand.

You want to take him home; you want to do anything else but what you have to do. He's still asleep, it should be easy, like putting a child to rest. But you tremble, and you can't do it.

Frantic steps, she runs along the cemetery lane. She runs and she sees him. She begs you not to hurt him, don't hurt your son —her son. This must be madness and you have to stop. She sees the blood on his lips, it's fresh and she knows. You don't beg her to believe you; you don't want to believe either.

He wakes up like a nightmare, the eyes on his face aren't really your wife's eyes, not anymore. You want to reach for him, hug him, help him, while he tries to crawl out of the tomb like a lizard. Your wife calls him; she calls him like he was just back from a mischievous stroll. She begs him to recognize her. Your son, who doesn't move like your son, who's still too weak and sleepy to crawl out of his tomb, he looks at her in all his reptilian slowness. She's so close and you don't know how to do what you have to do.

He looks at you. The eyes on his face aren't really your wife's eyes, not anymore. You want to reach for him, hug him, help him, while he crawls out of the tomb like a lizard. She takes the stake from your hand, looking at your son in the eyes, slowly she calls his name. He doesn't seem to remember; a half-forgotten dream of his consciousness, that's what she hoped for. But that's a nightmare.

He bares his teeth, fully awake. He's snapping now. You hurry to take her away, but it is too late. The stake has already found its way to his heart. He dies again as he was born, looking your wife in the eyes. And in the last moment, he's looking at you both with eyes which still are the same colour of the night sky, and that hurts like nothing before.

He's your boy and here he lies. With a broken heart.

She laughs and laughs, her hands dirty with blood. She laughs and laughs and she says she would have never let you do it. And she laughs, the queen of all the laughs while she clutches onto your arms and you help her to move. She laughs and laughs as she places a kiss on your boy's cheek and you seal again the grave. She clutches you the whole way home, afraid and stricken by grief like you, trembling like you, laughing and laughing until she is home and she doesn't laugh anymore. Or cry anymore. Or talk. Or walk.

Your son's wife-to-be in a couple of days is dead and gone, with her soul intact. But a heart can break from loss and pain, and lack of blood. In the newspaper you read rumors of a vampire lady allegedly killed in Styria. You know it's not just folktales.

Your wife sits by the window day by day. When she speaks, she babbles like a dream half remembered. You call out your lessons for a while. You get rid of any sharp object after the first time she tries to kill herself, she looks at you like being alive is a punishment. She never judged you, with your son's eyes. You keep saying it's not her fault your son is dead, she hasn't done anything evil and wrong, she didn't do wrong, she has to heal and be alright, it's not her fault (you know the fault is yours alone, you should have known better). But she isn't alright. She doesn't babble anymore, she gets violent, against everything and everyone. You don't sleep anymore, and you feel on the verge of madness and heartbreak too. Your heart is still broken, you're already dead, and maybe mad. She doesn't mind anything anymore, not even you. Not even herself.

You faint one day, from fatigue and worry, but you persist. You can't afford to keep her home and you know it, but this breaks you even more. You can't let her by herself, but you need to work and sleep and to know she's alive and well, even if she seems already dead.

A student of yours and his wife run an all-female sanatorium. She will be in good hands, you keep on saying to yourself, she would be safe like she would be at home. You leave her with people who love her, who care for you both, there would be garlic flowers out of the window and books on the shelves (she doesn't read anymore), she will be safe. She doesn't seem to mind; she doesn't seem to mind anything and anyone. As she's dead, as you are. You go to her every week, save a certain long summer and autumn.

But it's almost winter and you come back. The younglings at your side, like ducklings behind an old coot.

He's the first one to come in, blue eyes like your son had. He kneels in front of your wife, while you hold her. He speaks softly, trying to reassure her, telling her a bit of his tale. Then she seems to remember something, or she's looking for it. She caresses young Arthur's cheek with the faintest smile, almost fearing to break him. Two words, a voice so worn out, a bit less un-dead, just a little bit, a phantom of herself, but more like herself: "He resembles..."

You hold her even closer, while the young Harkers and Jack peep in the sunlit room, and wave their hands almost shyly to greet. Madame Mina smiles, warmly like she did one day in another asylum. You keep your wife close while you explain to her that those younglings are all in desperate need of a mother, including Jack here, and that from now on things would get better for everyone, because they all know and understand and to know and understand is to love.

And while Madame Mina and the others tell their tale, you know that deep somewhere, even for the faintest moments, your wife isn't dead or un-dead. She's alive. Like your son. Your joy, blue night in their eyes. For all of your days and evermore.

Ever blooming.

Noemi Novembre graduated in Languages, Cultures and Modern Literature from the University of Studies of Bari, that's a lively city in Italy, currently taking a Master Degree in Modern Philology (because Knights of the Round Table are cool). Being born and living in an Italian sun-kissed, sea-blessed city, she naturally developed a love for all things gothic, spooky and/or British (Bilbo Baggins, Jonathan Harker and Catherine Morland are her life's role models). She has published several short tales as a young adult, for some literary competition: she's really fond of the one which is an urban fantasy retelling of Red Riding Hood, and the one narrated by a judgmental black cat living in XIX century Paris.

Van Helsing's Guests
By Kay Hanifen

LETTER, ABRAHAM VAN HELSING
TO JONATHAN AND MINA HARKER

11 January 1910

My Dear Madame Mina and Jonathan,

I know you have received my telegram telling you of young Quincey and Lucy's safe arrival three days ago, but I know you must be eager to receive a proper letter telling you of their adventures in Amsterdam. And I know it must be a shock that they will be hand delivering it to you. Unfortunately, I have been called out of town and must pause their apprenticeships until I return.

That said, you will be gladdened to know that they have done well in assisting this old man in his practice. Young Quincey is as bright as his father and just as gentle. He has his mother's kindness and bedside manner, immediately soothing the most agitated of patients. And Jonathan, you would be so proud of the way he guards his little sister, even if she might chafe under some of his protectiveness. Lucy is, of course, just as much a bright spark as her mother: clever, kind, and always two steps ahead. Both are incredibly quick studies, and Jack has taught them well.

It is unusual for me to take on an apprentice, let alone two and let alone a girl on the cusp of womanhood, but this is a new century, and Lucy has the potential to be as great a physician as any man. Because she is so young, though, we will take it slow. No madmen or zoophagi. She will witness and observe, and when the time comes, I will fight for her place in medical schools.

I met them at the Amsterdam docks, and goodness, I hardly recognized the pair. It had been far too long since I last saw them, and they had grown quite a bit. Quincey has shot up like the weeds, and Lucy is the spitting image of her mother.

When she spotted me, she ran up and threw her arms around me, kissing my cheek. I staggered backwards with the force of her affection. "Uncle Abraham! How I've missed you!"

I patted her back and pressed a kiss to her forehead. "I have missed you too, dear girl. Let me get a good look at you." I stepped back slightly to take her in. It feels like just yesterday I held her in my arms as she babbled her baby babble. And now she was going to shadow me as an apprentice.

Quincey was more hesitant. He bowed stiffly, but that would not do.

"Come here, my boy. Give this old man a hug. Neither of us know how many I have left."

The boy laughed, relaxing and embracing me. "I have missed you, Uncle Abraham."

"And I you, young man. Are you both ready to learn at my side?" I stepped back, taking him in. It's strange to see him so grown when I did not have the chance with my own boy. Jonathan and Mina, I have always thought of you and Arthur and Jack as my children and they my grandchildren, but it is a sweet kind of sadness to watch this boy become a man when mine could not.

"Uncle, we have been learning at your side since we were small," Quincey replied, picking up their shared trunk. "This is simply more formalized."

I chuckled at that. "Right you are, my boy. Now come. I will get you settled. Tomorrow, we will make our rounds, and you both will get to see firsthand my methods."

The children's faces lit up with delight, and we made our way to my home. I confess that these last few years have been lonely, with the rest of you so busy and me slowing down in my career. So, it is so wonderful to hear the sound of laughter in my home once more, and the children (though they are not truly children anymore) have brought great joy.

Both immediately lost themselves in my library, exclaiming over various medical illustrations and sketches of wildlife from exotic lands. I watched them indulgently as the maid brought in their tea.

Then, young Lucy pulled out a tome of a different source: "*Strigoi, Lycanthropy, and Other Esoteric Afflictions?*" Her eyes widened. "Uncle Abraham, is this one of the books you referenced when battling the fiend who killed Aunt Lucy and Uncle Quincey?"

"Quite so," I said, plucking the book from her grasp, much to her dismay. "And this is not for the eyes of a girl your age."

"But what if we encounter a vampire?" she protested. "Shouldn't we know what to look for? When Mother tells the story, she always says that staying in ignorance—even if it is meant to protect you—is a greater danger than any awful truth."

"I agree with Lucy," Quincey said, not even bothering to hide his naked curiosity when looking at the book. "It is better that we know and are prepared than to be kept in the dark."

Mina, these are truly your children. Curious, clever, and logical as any great man. I could not help but indulge them. "You may read it, but remember that the vampire may be real, but it is also exceedingly rare to encounter one. In my many decades on earth, the only one I ever had the displeasure of meeting was Dracula." I turned to address Quincey specifically. "You are young and brash, like all boys on the cusp of manhood are. I do not wish to fill your head with foolishly gallant ideas. This book is to arm you with knowledge, but you must never seek out a vampire. Am I understood?"

"Yes, Uncle," Quincey replied.

Lucy remained silent, but I doubted she would ever attempt something so mad. It is usually the boys who are foolish like that. So, we drank our tea and they sat close together, sharing the book as they parsed out the Latin words.

The next day, we made our rounds. Our first stop was a man in an insane asylum, one known for his strange spells of breaking with reality. His name was T. Hutter. He was a young man, only a few years older than Quincey. Most days out of the month, he was calm and quiet, the sanest man you would ever meet. We would let him out for that period. He would go home and lives a quiet, ordinary life.

But every full moon, he would convince himself that he was a werewolf and check himself back into the hospital. He would howl and snarl and crawl on all fours for three days, snapping at orderlies, only eating raw meat, and screaming that no one come any closer for fear that he would spread his curse. And then, once the moon began to wane, he was back to normal. He is no true lycanthrope, but he had a sort of lycanthropy of the mind. For the most part, he is harmless. Even with the threat of the snapping jaws, he does not truly bite. During these full moon periods, I would attempt to remind him that he is a man, but little progress had been made.

For her safety, Lucy stayed back while Quincey and I approached. The patient sat curled in the corner, snarling and snapping his teeth.

"Mr. Hutter, it is nice to see you. How are you feeling this morning?" I asked. "I have brought a few pet students if that is acceptable to you."

"Tell them to stay back," he growled. "I am not safe to be around."

Though I kept approaching, Quincey stopped. "My uncle says that you believe you are a werewolf. That sounds very frightening."

"Then you should stay away."

Quincey shook his head emphatically. "I meant that it sounds very frightening for you. I know I would be afraid if I was certain that I could lose control and hurt my sister." He gestured to Lucy standing behind him. "What makes you think you are a werewolf?"

"My teeth have grown sharp. I can feel it in my mouth. And I am growing claws."

"Can I check?" Quincey asked, approaching slowly and kneeling in front of the patient. "May I see your hands?"

Reluctantly, he offered them. Quincey hummed and examined the fingernails. "They look like ordinary human hands to me. What about you, Professor?"

"Those hands are definitely a human's," I replied, surprised by Quincey's bedside manner. I had reached a brick wall using facts and logic, but Hutter seemed to be responding to Quincey's approach.

"And may I see your teeth?" the boy asked, and Hutter opened his mouth wide. "Well, I don't see any fangs, but I'm not an expert. Uncle?"

"No fangs. Just simple human teeth."

Hutter seemed to relax at that. "That is good to hear. I must transform back into a man during the daytime."

"We can check on you again tonight," Quincey offered. "We can confirm if you are a man or a beast."

Hutter broke out into a wide, relieved smile. "Thank you, dear boy. That will be most helpful."

"Would you like to try your food cooked today then?" Quincey asked. "We can test if your stomach remains human."

Hutter pondered for a moment. "I suppose it cannot hurt."

"We'll see to it that you get your morning meal, then," he said, getting to his feet.

Once we had left the cell, I clapped the boy on the back. "I am impressed, young man. I have never seen a patient so quickly soothed."

Quincey shrugged, looking bashful. "Father once said that the greatest thing for his recovery was being believed. We know that he is no lycanthrope, but it is a fact for him. I—I simply listened, I suppose, and tried to reassure him that he was not the danger he believed himself to be."

"When did this first start?" Lucy asked, scribbling into her notebook with the seriousness of a man twice her age.

"After a journey to a small Hungarian village. He claimed he met a nobleman who kept a pet wolf, which bit him. After that, he became convinced that the wolf was, in fact, a werewolf, and it passed its curse onto him."

Lucy stopped short. "And you don't think this sounds similar to Father's story."

Perhaps it had been a mistake to allow her to read the book after all.

"I agree. It is. But he is not showing any true signs of lycanthropy, not like your namesake, who was dying in a way that could not be understood by modern science. Lucy's blood would vanish every night. Her condition improved when we gave her protection against the vampire, and in the later stages of her affliction, her gums receded and her teeth sharpened as her personality changed. Hutter is a poor man in pain, but his delusions are little more than products of his troubled mind."

She still seemed hesitant to believe me, so I gave her shoulder a squeeze. "Lucy, you have a bright mind, and you have made some excellent connections, but do you remember what your English detective once said?"

"Once you eliminate the impossible, whatever remains, however improbable, must be the answer," she recited.

"Yes. Science is about eliminating the impossible and understanding the conditions for the improbable. We know better than most that there is more possible than the rest of the world would believe, but we must first look to the body and the mind to treat scientifically before we assume the supernatural. If you hear hoofbeats in the night, what is more likely: a horse or a unicorn?"

"A horse," she replied.

"And if you find a horn embedded in a tree, then you know it is a unicorn. But without the horn, it is safe to assume a horse passed you by. Do you understand?"

She nodded, a small furrow forming in her brows. "Yes, Uncle."

The rest of the rounds were uneventful. We performed house calls, checking on children with fevers (with Quincey and Lucy keeping their distance, of course), expectant mothers, work injuries, and old ladies with nervous conditions. Your children behaved admirably throughout and were of immense help to this old man.

We returned home after a long, full day, ate our supper, and went to bed, too exhausted for much else. And we have been maintaining the routine for the past few days. You should be very proud of your darlings.

But unfortunately, as I said, I have been called on a case out of town and will be sending them home in three days from the time of writing this letter. They will be able to explain the rest.

All my love,
Abraham Van Helsing

Abraham Van Helsing's Diary

14 January 1910.—I am rather ashamed that I was not entirely honest with the Harker's, but I did not wish to worry them, as they have already suffered greatly.

We returned to the cell of Mr. Hutter on the first night. When we arrived, he was in the throes of his "transformation," crying out and contorting himself like an epileptic. I had witnessed this before but never so severely, and I regretted bringing the children. They may be mature, but it was difficult for one of any age to see a man in such agony.

"Mister Hutter," Quincey exclaimed, rushing to the man's side before I could stop him.

"Stay back," Hutter growled, swiping at him. Though Hutter's nails were cut to the quick by his own request, boy staggered away from him in surprise.

"Mister Hutter," he said again.

The man snarled and howled before seizing once more in a painful looking fit. "No, Orlok, please! Don't!"

This was the worst fit of lycanthropic delusion I had ever seen from him. His muscles clenched and shook, the tendons in his neck standing out like ropes as his eyes rolled back in his head.

"Orlok?" Lucy repeated, scribbling in her notebook. "Was that the name of the count whose pet bit him?"

"He has never said the man's name," I replied. "Aside from explaining the bite, we could not get him to speak of the incident. He seemed to feel much shame around it." I had dismissed Lucy earlier that day, but I wondered if she may, in fact, be seeing something I had failed to notice. I was insistent that the supernatural was not at the root of this, perhaps because I wished for it to be so.

Quincey knelt in front of the poor man. "Mister Hutter, what do you see right now?"

"Death," he sobbed as he scratched at his skin. "Hunger and death. My pack runs through the forest, searching for food in the bleak winter. We stumble upon a farmer and tear him to shreds. His blood melts the snow, and I lap it up, preferring it to flesh. It sates me for now, but I will be hungry again soon. So, I'm slowly moving closer, mile by mile with the pack until I reach someplace where they have no more reason to fear that which lurks in the night."

Quincey looked back up at me, his brows furrowed. And I knew he was remembering the stories his mother told of using her connection to Dracula to spy on him as he had spied on her. Perhaps this Orlok had fed on him and formed an unintentional and unusually strong connection. It would explain the cyclical nature of his affliction.

And as suddenly as the seizures began, they ceased. Hutter curled in the corner growling unintelligibly and there was nothing we could do to coax words from him again. Much like Madame Mina's affliction, his "transformations" occurred at dawn and dusk. He would remain in this state for the rest of the night and would become verbal again at sunrise.

I took the children from the room. Both seemed to be thinking what I was thinking. I turned to Lucy and took her by the shoulders. "Madame, I beg your forgiveness. There is a good chance that you were correct in your initial assessment."

"Orlok was a name in your book of the undead," she said. "Like Dracula, he was a student of the Scholomance, and it was said that when he died, the Devil didn't wish to let him go, so he turned the lord into a vampire."

"I suppose I must brush up on that book," I said. "You, my dear Lucy, are as bright as your mother." I turned to Jonathan, who was still watching Hutter through the window to his cell. Taking him by the shoulder, I led him away. "And you have your mother's gentle compassion. We cannot help him now, but if it is a vampire at the center of his affliction, we will defeat him as we did Dracula."

"Will you try again at dawn?" Quincey asked.

"I will. In the meantime, you and your sister should focus on getting your rest. We have another long day of rounds tomorrow, and now we must rise even earlier to speak with him at dawn."

We found him twitching and seizing the next morning. "Mister Hutter," Quincey said, taking the lead. I am impressed with that boy and his ability to soothe the poor man's suffering. If something was to go wrong, I would step in, but Mr. Hutter seemed to respond to him better than any doctor. "Can you tell me what you see?"

"I am in a cave. There is something affixed to my neck. It smells of dirt and I cannot sleep without it. I have taken shelter there for the day while my pack hunts for their preferred food. We are moving closer to civilization, where I will walk among mankind once more. But for now, I am sated by the blood of the farmer and need to rest like a tick glutted on blood." And like a marionette with his strings cut, the man collapsed, panting and exhausted from his night of suffering. He blinked up at us, his expression shifting from confusion to anxiety. "It's you again. Have I grown claws? Are my teeth sharp?"

"No," Quincey said. "I don't see either."

"Mister Hutter," Lucy piped up as she carefully approached. "You said a name last night. Orlok. Was this the nobleman whose wolf bit you? Can you tell us what happened?"

He furrowed his brows. "I remember so little of that journey. All I remember is the bite and the pain and the fever that came after. But Orlok is his name. Yes. Orlok. I was lost on a journey to the Black Sea for a business trip when I stumbled upon his castle. He took me in, and he was charming, welcoming. I remember being so proud to tell him of our business, how this was the first time my father gave me such an important task, and I was eager to prove myself to him. He listened with such attentiveness. But then he…" Hutter went pale. "I don't know. I cannot remember what changed, only terror and the pain of the bite."

"You were only bitten once, correct?" I asked.

Hutter pulled up his shirtsleeve to reveal the scar on his wrist. "Just once. But that is all it takes to spread a werewolf's curse, is it not?"

I glanced over at the children. "Perhaps it is time for you to step out for the sake of Mr. Hutter's privacy."

"But—" Lucy began to protest, but Quincey squeezed her shoulder and led her to the door.

"As you wish, sir."

I waited until they were gone before I spoke. "As the English saying goes, I have good news and bad news. The good news is that you are not a werewolf. The bad news is that you have been bitten by a vampire, one that prefers his wolf form. The bite created a psychic connection, as they all do, but it seems this Orlok was unaware of the strength of the one he formed with you, likely because he bit you on the full moon."

Hutter blinked. "What the devil are you talking about?"

I told him the story of the battle with the Count Dracula and the symptoms I observed in Madame Mina and Miss Lucy. When I finished, he asked, "And those are the children of your friends? Will they be coming along?"

"No. I am sending them home while we face vampire ourselves. Orlok seems to have embraced his animal instincts, but he still has the great mind of a scholar of the dark arts. It is too dangerous for them. But with your youthful strength and my experience, we can find and slay Orlok."

The children were unsurprisingly unhappy with this decision when I told them after we returned home. "But Uncle, we can help," Lucy protested.

I patted her curls. "I know you can. But it's too dangerous."

"And it isn't too dangerous for you?" Quincey asked, crossing his arms. "I do not mean to offend, but you are not young anymore."

"It's true. I have lived long, but you are young. You have your whole lives ahead of you, and I'll never forgive myself if you two came to harm." I winked. "And your mother and father would murder me and make sure the body is never found." It was an attempt to lighten the mood, but the two were not amused. I sighed. "I am afraid I must bring down the law. You will go home while Hutter and I deal with Orlok and that is final. We will resume your apprenticeships when I return."

"*If* you return," Lucy muttered, her eyes glistening with tears. Quincey too looked as though he may cry but kept the British stiff upper lip.

It is better this way. I am an old man, and I am at peace with my end, but I cannot bear it for the rest.

After three days of sullenness, I saw them off at the docks for their journey back to London by ferry. Despite their irritation, they still hugged me tight when we said goodbye.

I will miss them, their laughter and their brightness. It is easy to forget how alone I am when they are around. I suppose it is a comfort to know that, should I not survive this adventure, I will see my wife and my boy again.

30 January 1910.—What a miracle true friends are. After I sent the children away, Hutter and I prepared for our journey. At dawn and dusk, I would hypnotize the man as I did Madame Mina and learn of Orlok's movements. We would also scour the newspapers, searching for stories of any suspicious rashes of animal attacks where wolves no longer live. Once we had narrowed it to the closest city, we began our journey there.

Despite the terror, there is something invigorating to the blood when on an adventure. I felt twenty years younger as we took a train to the small village of Murnau, where a series of mutilations at the hands of wolves had paralyzed the town with terror. Hutter reminded me of Jonathan Harker when we first met: a gallant, young man who has faced a nightmare and come out the other end made of true grit. He made for excellent company on our journey.

It was easier to gain information from Hutter than it was with Madame Mina, likely because the vampire was unaware of the connection.

The night we arrived, I hypnotized him and had him search through Orlok's eyes for any identifiable landmarks in the woods surrounding the town. "There is a cave," he said. "It is partially covered by a boulder, but there is still space for a pack of large wolves to slip in and out."

So, in the daylight, that was what we were to look for. The next morning, we began our quest, trudging through the woods at the break of dawn, searching for the cave he described, for Orlok almost certainly slept there with his homeland's dirt around his neck. We were armed, of course, with holy water, stakes, blades, crucifixes, a paste I had made of the host, and guns. Anything to battle true wolves and vampires alike.

As the sun began to go down, Hutter let out an exclamation of excitement. "There! I see it!"

"Come, come. We have very little time." Despite my own tiredness from trudging over snowy ground all day, I urged him forward.

When we reached the mouth of the cave, though, Hutter froze, going pale. Around us, wolves began to howl. "He is awake."

Orlok did not so much emerge from the shadows as separate from them, a horrific apparition made flesh. He was less human than Dracula, with a long face and longer teeth that filled his mouth. His mustache and brows were furry, but the top of his head was bald in patches, revealing pointed ears. Long fingers with even longer claws scraped the side of the cave wall. Under his neck, he wore a box. This must have been where he kept the dirt of his homeland so that he could travel more easily.

"You dare attempt to kill me in my slumber," Orlok growled. His gaze locked in on Hutter as he approached, a smirk forming. "Or have you come back for more. Was my kiss not enough?"

The man beside me froze in place like a statue. Suddenly, he looked young, younger than Quincey, and vulnerable. "I—I didn't."

"You gave so willingly last time."

"I didn't want it," Hutter insisted. "I never wanted it."

"So, you aren't here to offer more of your free will. A pity. Regardless, you have brought me and my brethren a convenient meal." All around us, eyes glowed in the light of dusk.

I pulled my crucifix from the inside of my coat and held it out as the vampire hissed and backed deeper into the cave. "Hutter, I have a box in my bag. Take it and smear its contents along the entrance to the cave to seal it."

"Yes, sir." I felt him reach into my bag and pull it out. He then rushed forward and spread the paste I made from the host onto the floor of the entrance. "What will that do?" he asked, rejoining me and drawing his gun.

"It will trap him there. Even if we do not survive, he will be unable to escape as long as the line remains unbroken."

"Will that help with the wolves?" Hutter asked, watching anxiously as the creatures approached, snarling and sniffing the air.

"Probably not."

"Oh."

Orlok stood behind us and checked his nails, seemingly unconcerned. "The only reason why they haven't attacked is because I am curious as to how you found me, Thomas."

"I'm afraid you will die disappointed, fiend." I raised my gun and fired, shooting the vampire in the head. Though I knew it would likely do nothing, a part of me hoped that shooting the vampire would cause the wolves to break from his control and flee.

It did not.

Orlok staggered backward in surprise but remained upright, grinning and revealing his sharp teeth. "So, it is to be like this. My children of the night, come and feast!"

The wolves charged, and Hutter and I fired off our revolvers in quick succession, taking several. But soon, we were out of bullets and the wolves were circling.

"I am sorry that it will end like this, Mr. Hutter," I said.

"I am simply glad to die knowing that I am sane," he replied, and we drew our knives, preparing to fight to the end.

But then gunshots reported through the air. The sound of footsteps resounded on the icy snow as Arthur, Jonathan, Quincey, and Jack all barreled towards us. I took advantage of the wolves' distraction to remove my flask of holy water and splash the vampire with it. He staggered backwards with a cry, his skin bubbling and burning. This was enough to momentarily break his concentration when controlling the wolves.

"Hutter, now!" I shouted, drawing my stake. He did the same and charged, piercing the vampire's chest with a wooden stake. Jack dismounted and rushed to us, holding the vampire down as we hammered it in, piercing his heart. I took the knife and with Jack's assistance, chopped off Orlok's head. Once the deed was done, I embraced my former student. "How did you know where to find us?" I exclaimed.

"Quincey and Lucy told us everything as soon as they returned home, you old fool," he replied, embracing me with equal ferocity. "Then, it was simply a matter of Mina finding your notes and figuring out that you were going here. We were searching the woods, and when we heard gunshots and wolves, we came running."

I shook my head in pleased disbelief. Of course she figured it out. Madame Mina was always the best of us.

Jack stepped back to take a better look at me. "Are you hurt?"

"No, I am quite fine."

"Then you are in for the scolding if a lifetime—not just from me but Madame Mina, Arthur, Jonathan, Lucy, *and* Quincey. What were you thinking going alone?"

"That I am an old man, and you have been through enough. And besides, I wasn't alone. I had Mister Hutter." I gestured to the young man, who was chatting eagerly with Quincey. "He needed to face this demon and conquer it just as you did with Dracula."

Jack shook his head, somewhere between amused and exasperated. "You both are very lucky to be alive."

I embraced him once more, throwing my arm around his shoulder and leading him to rejoin the others. "No, I am lucky to have such friends as you." I may have made peace with death, but life, as always, remains worth living.

Kay Hanifen was born on a Friday the 13th and once lived for three months in a haunted castle. So, obviously, she had to become a horror writer. Her work has appeared in over 150 anthologies and magazines. Her first anthology as an editor, *Till the Yule Log Burns Out*, was published in 2024. Her first novel, *The Last Ballard*, debuted in 2025. When she's not consuming pop culture with the voraciousness of a vampire at a 24-hour blood bank, you can usually find her with her black cats or at:

kayhanifenauthor.wordpress.com.

Instagram: https://www.instagram.com/katharinehanifen/

A Change of Perspective
By Bill Cozza

Atop a great hill overlooking Dublin, nestled in a ridge of mountains sits a stone sentinel. A derelict reflection of a bygone age. A burned and forgotten relic. A place where monsters dwell and the devil himself is said to have visited. A disturbed sacred site, shielded by forestry, the fortress looks down upon the city with bemused charm and hellish contempt. Its original name lost to history, Montpelier Hill is a site of debauchery, ritual, and exploration. And as such sites tend to do, it calls out and draws in explorers. Pipe smoke scents the air as a traveler observes Dublin by full moonlight beyond the Hell Fire Club of Montpelier. Following an encounter within, a renowned monster hunter will soon find his self-certainty in question.

Monster hunter?" Abraham Van Helsing laughed. "*Ja,* some people have been prone to exaggeration." His tone elicited chuckles from the auditorium as intended, hesitant laughter separating those who came as students of science and those who came to hear fantastical tales. "It is true and I will not deny that I was involved in some extraordinary events. You know this, I know it is why some of you are here. But my friends, I must remind you that I am a *doctor*. A scientist. A doctor, perhaps, with experience that other doctors will refuse to acknowledge, and experiences that are…what is the word? Controversial?"

His Dutch accent played in the air, the students couldn't help but feel drawn to him, amused by him. The controversial events in question had made Dr. Van Helsing notorious in England and the attention had become so heavy that he felt forced to return to Holland. In some circles his credentials had been in question, but in the ensuing fifteen years, he maintained respect as a physician…and a metaphysician, though he'd had no further publicized encounters with the "extraordinary." Still, he drew crowds wherever he was invited to speak. Abraham hoped that at least half of those crowds were more interested in his scientific lectures than his much more documented exploits. He was not naïve, however, and he knew his reputation as one of the leading experts in monsters and the occult. He could spot the difference easily enough in the audience, and the students and faculty of Trinity College were no different.

"You must remember, because I know many of you are here to hear about the vampire, I was a doctor first, and I am a doctor still. I simply have what you call an open mind. I was asked to consult on the case of Miss Westenra from the perspective of a blood disorder, *ja?*" These many years after, it still hurt to speak of Miss Lucy, the bright light that he had failed. Not a day passed that she was not on his mind, nor her dear friends, who were now (at least he hoped still) *his* dear friends. "This is what I have come to talk to you about today, not that case, but the necessity for scientists to keep an open mind. My former student Jack and I only arrived at what some have called an unnatural solution to Miss Westenra's case when presented with irrefutable proof. We exhausted all known options, intervened with every scientific method, examined every possible cause. Only when that cause exceeded any scientific explanation did we accept what we were seeing. Because science must evolve!"

He saw shifting glances from some of the elder students and he recognized the doubt. He understood the doubt; these were some of the brightest scientific minds in Europe after all. Trinity

College had a strong science focus and encouraged students to trust only what they could see and prove. "Look at you, look where you are. Scientific advancement thrives here. This is the school that spawned the creator of the hypodermic needle. William Hershcel discovered Uranus using what he learned here! And just a few years ago, Mr. Thomson discovered the…what did he call it? The electron, yes. I know Cambridge wants to take credit for that, but Thomson is one of *you*. These things do not happen without thinking outside of what science has already discovered. We must keep testing, pushing, exploring. And to do that, we must open our minds. This is how Pasteur learned to prevent rabies. But what did people say about his vaccinations? Another *controversy*. There is always pushback to scientific and medical advancement."

He paused, allowing his words to echo in the chamber, took a drink of his water before he continued. "We seek to understand that which others deny. When confronted with truth, even when others deny the truth, we as scientists trust the evidence. Whether that evidence is the efficacy of inoculation—and trust me, the world will eventually see the importance of that advancement; or they will regret it—or whether that evidence is that a creature that *shouldn't* exist *does*, it does not behoove us to deny it. After all, what some call unnatural is simply that which has not yet been discovered. If it exists, it is natural, we just might not understand it yet. Open minds, my friends, is what science is supposed to be about."

Van Helsing took some time to answer questions as he prepared to wrap up his lecture, not only because his time was growing short and lately he couldn't afford to overstay his welcome. But here he was at Trinity College, and he longed to see the Long Room. His academic mind dreamed of that massive library. He'd been afforded some quality time to peruse it, and a private showing of the Book of Kells.

"Before I close, I know what many of you want. I will answer exactly one vampire question."

A cacophony of yelps as half a room of hands flew up.

"*Ongelofelijk!*" the professor exhaled. Then he picked a hand at random, one belonging to a young redhead, her pale face highlighted by freckles.

"Thank you, Professor," she smiled. "I'm curious how you describe the nature of a vampire? Do they show any diversity or are they a uniform species?"

Both intrigued and perplexed, Abraham considered the question for a moment before confidently declaring their nature as inherent evil. He reminded everyone that his experience was mostly academic aside from the few he'd encountered in the past. But both his research and his firsthand experience told him that these creatures *were* intrinsically evil, soulless affronts to the Lord. He'd never encountered a case to consider otherwise. The Transylvanian, he told them, was the closest thing to the Devil on Earth he'd ever imagined, and each of his brides were animals. He stopped a moment to remember Mina and her kind, loving nature, even through the darkness, but he had to remember that Mina had not fully transformed. So, he concluded, a vampire could never live a civilized life and would always be bound by their murderous thirst.

His lecture ended with thunderous applause and he excused himself, shaking hands with those who stopped him on his way out of the lecture hall. He smirked when one of the students even asked him to autograph a copy of Mr. Stoker's novel. That book, though the full and true accounts of the encounter with the Transylvanian, never stopped haunting him. But it brought young people joy, so he indulged them whenever this happened, telling himself this was the closest to danger these young people would come, and they enjoyed feeling part of the adventure in some way by being near him. He couldn't deny them that, although he wished he could convince them to take the lesson of the book to be that they shouldn't *want* to be close to the adventure or the danger. He caught sight of the redhead who'd asked him the closing question, and she solemnly nodded her thanks to him. He nodded back and left the room, on his way to one of the most famous libraries in the world.

The Long Room was an academic's dream. Its impressive length, for which it was named, housed countless rows of shelves on two stories, beneath a beautiful wooden vaulted ceiling. Hundreds of thousands of volumes filled this room, along with busts of great thinkers. Abraham had seldom seen its like, and he took his time admiring the space. He had already perused the collection and had examined some of the texts over a distant table when he felt his bones weary and needed to walk about.

He admired another treasure of the Long Room for a while, the Brian Boru Harp. A beautifully etched oak harp, this had once been said to have been owned by the High King of Ireland. Though that claim was later disproven, the harp itself provided the template for the nation's emblem. It was an impressive instrument, without a doubt. When he returned to his table, Van Helsing found a book there that he had not picked for himself. It lay open atop his stack, as though someone had left something for him to see, though he'd not seen anyone approach. Curious, the old man sat down to see what had been left for him. It wouldn't be the first time someone had tried to get his attention in secret. And as he read, he did find himself intrigued.

The passage before him described an old hunting lodge in the Dublin Mountains just outside the city. Montpelier, better known now as the Hell Fire Club. It had been constructed, so the book told him, around 1725 by William Conolly, who had ordered the destruction of an ancient burial cairn to construct the building. He'd even had some of the stones from the cairn used in the construction itself. A splendid idea, Abraham imagined. Many strange happenings were reported at Montpelier, and superstition attributed them to the disturbance of the cairn. The lodge's roof had been destroyed multiple times, but what people talked about most were the happenings inside the lodge. This had become a meeting place for affluent men to allegedly take part in debauched acts. Drinking, sex, ritual sacrifices, and devil worship were all said to take place at the lodge. Local folklore even told of a night the Devil showed up to join in a card game before vanishing in a ball of flame. There was the story of a priest who found the club members sacrificing a black cat and who then exorcised a demon from the cat's corpse. Or of a lord who traded his soul to the Devil to wipe out his debts, only to distract the Devil at Montpelier and flee. Or the alleged kidnapping, killing, and cannibalizing of a farmer's daughter by the group. All the stories of black masses and sacrifices to Satan were of course unproven urban legend. But the lodge had been burned out in a fire, that much was proven. And there it remained, atop its hill, a supposed supernatural hotspot. Whoever had left this for him to read, Van Helsing had to admit, had succeeded in getting his attention. It seemed worth a trip, if only for the hike and the promised view of the city.

The moon had risen, full and pale, by the time Abraham finished his hike to the summit of Montpelier Hill illuminating his view of the city below and the mountains around him. It had not been an arduous hike, but it was enough for Van Helsing—a man in his mid-sixties—to question his choices. He found the stone lodge before him and paused to gather himself.

The lodge was smaller than the legends had led him to expect, but it had an air of menacing aristocracy. The stonework was masterful, but its blackened façade and charred roof beckoned ominously to the observer. Its once brilliant design now burned out and forsaken. There was a distinct lack of woodland noise on this spot, the professor noted. As he circled the structure, admiring it and taking measure of it, he came to the ancient stonework that had once laid the foundation of the erstwhile cairn, no more now than jagged stones jutting up from the earth like castrated fangs. From their placement, he could tell the burial mound must have been enormous. He wondered which stones in the building had come from here. Curiosity pulling him along, the professor entered the Hell Fire Club, wrapping his rosary around his fist. The professor was not stupid, after all, of course he came prepared. He had his rosary, a stake, a knife, and a vial of holy water.

Its inside was more obviously scorched. Rooms led into each other, indistinguishable from each other, and there was nothing to see but some rubble, cramped quarters, and the occasional shallow storage space. The inside left much to be desired from this fabled place. As Abraham stood by a glassless window, he thought that through its notable eerie atmosphere, it was a wonderful location.

He admired the mountain view for a few moments before deciding to step outside. As if in reply to his mounting disappointment, he heard a faint rumbling as he turned from the window. There was a shuffling in the dirt across the room. Van Helsing trained his eyes on the darkened alcove, but he could hardly see that corner in the gloom. He felt his sweat turn cold, the late autumn air freezing it as it dripped down his back. His breath quickened as he realized it was not rumbling he heard, but a growl.

Abraham fumbled in his coat pocket, past his pipe, and pulled his matches.

He struck one and the flare immediately revealed a pair of glowing eyes. Beneath them, ravenous teeth. The figure before him must have crawled out from one of the storage spaces, as he'd not seen or heard a trace of it as he inspected the building.

But here it stood, skeletal and ravaged, every limb stretched and sinewy. It was sparsely clothed, swimming in what it did wear, its skin was gray and bruised, and tufts of hair clung to its head in patches. Its fingers were elongated and tipped with bloody talon-like nails. These and the vicious teeth hanging from its gaping maw told the professor that this was a vampire, but this was a devastated one, weathered and mad. Not at all like the sophisticated creatures he'd encountered in London and Transylvania. There was no language in this face, no intelligence in these eyes, only the hunger. The deep hunger.

Van Helsing's match died and the creature rushed him. Its mouth snapped ferociously as it shoved him against the wall. Winded and dizzy, he could only focus on those enormous teeth before him. His hand moved independently and flashed the rosary in front of him.

It squealed at him, baring its teeth, and hurled him across the room. The professor, not as young as he used to be, struggled to his feet slowly, winded. He was closer to the front door now and he slowly backed toward it, hoping to get the creature out in the open, in the moonlight, to see it more clearly.

But when he looked up, the creature had vanished.

Van Helsing quickened his pace out the door and circled the building, pulling the holy water and knife from his coat. As he walked, he looked for the creature by the front door. Seeing nothing, he rounded the corner, only to be surprised by the vampire crouching in the window hole. It pounced and pinned him to the ground, growling and slashing at his face. Its eyes blazed a hateful crimson as it snapped at him. He bucked underneath the creature, desperate to get an arm free while rivulets of blood fell, unleashed by those wild claws. This vampire had no trace of humanity in it, it was feral. When its head came down for another bite, Abraham crushed its nose with his forehead, finally gaining just enough freedom to smash his vial of holy water on its head.

Its skin boiled and cracked as it wailed, steam rising into the cool November air as it thrashed harder than before. Abraham struggled still to get free from its weight, until miraculously the monster was lifted from him. Air flooded the professor's lungs as the weight of the hideous thing left him. He watched as it soared into the air and landed hard near the foundation of the old cairn.

Beside him, he saw the redheaded student from his lecture. She had pulled the vampire from him and was dragging it by its neck. It snarled and swiped at her, kicking at the earth, but she maintained her grip, until finally she lifted it off the ground and slammed it back down hard over one of the jagged stones left from the cairn. The impact stopped its thrashing immediately as the creature's spine severed, but its bloody eyes still pierced, and its hungry mouth kept snapping.

Van Helsing rose and approached the creature, withdrawing his stake, the wood light in his hand. The vampire's still sizzling face let out a hiss as it tried and failed to defend itself before the professor's stake cracked its chest and stabbed its heart. Blood spurted in a short fountain before that mouth finally hung still.

There was no peace on this face in death, no return to what it had once been. The grotesquery before him remained. It was a relief when the girl cut off its head. A blur of her arm with a scythe of her own and it was over. What little blood remained trickled from its neck as its head rolled away toward the Hell Fire Club, as if trying to roll back to safety.

In the judgmental moonlight, the student wiped blood from her face and Abraham wiped blood from his hands.

"My name is Brigid," she said after she felt him staring. "I'm glad you got my message. C'mon down the hill, I'll buy you a pint."

He lit his pipe as she walked off into the shadows. Staring at Dublin below them, awash in pale light from the full moon, he contemplated her offer. She'd nearly gotten him killed, now she wanted to have a drink? He had no idea who she was, friend or enemy. But she'd gone through quite a bit to get his attention, and she'd ultimately saved him. Perhaps he could use that pint.

The Brazen Head was situated in the quays along the River Liffey, and bragged of being Ireland's oldest pub. Whether it was true of the country or not, it was indeed Dublin's oldest. It had been a pub since the 1750s and had existed as a coaching inn since the twelfth century. It had old world charm and made for a cozy environment for a chat with Brigid. She had waited for Van Helsing at the bottom of the hill and directed him here. They nestled into a booth in the corner with a couple pints of Guinness. There was a modest crowd, and a fiddler was playing traditional folksongs.

"I expected you'd be older," Brigid said abruptly, staring at him. Her red hair dangled in ringlets in front of bright green eyes. Her face had an intensity about it, and at the same time a softness that betrayed deep sadness.

"I get that often."

"I'm sorry for the cryptic library trick. I wasn't sure you'd go to the lodge if a young woman suggested it."

"I understand, but you could have warned me differently. You nearly got me killed." He sipped at his drink, trying to tamp down a flash of anger.

"Frankly, I expected you to be better prepared, too. I planned to follow you up whenever you went, I didn't expect it to be dusk. The stories about you made me imagine a great monster hunter." She fidgeted with her dress, picking at the hem of her sleeve, her nerves beginning to show.

Abraham exhaled sharply in derision. "I said already I am not a 'monster hunter.' I am a doctor. I was always a doctor. It was *one* experience."

"But you've become a legend…"

"Legends are stories. *Ja?* Tall tales. Everything I know about the extraordinary came from books!"

"But you do know the weaknesses and ways to kill vampires."

He shrugged. "Sure."

"What made you branch into metaphysics in the first place? Few doctors study what you call the extraordinary."

She was fidgeting more intensely; clearly, she was building up courage for something. But she'd asked a hard question, and Abraham felt his pulse quicken as he remembered. "I suppose it was because of my son. He'd be a grown man today, maybe have a family, a decent career. But he was taken from us too young." He swallowed a ball in his throat as he spoke. It had been ages since he spoke of his son. "After that, I went looking for…how would you say…proof of the supernatural. I thought if I could learn the signs, I might be able to communicate with him. Or I might at least find proof of a life beyond, to know he was at peace and safe." He blinked away a tear and Brigid looked on pityingly. "I never did find what I was looking for with him, but in my studies, I read about many creatures and legends from around the world. This is how, by the time Jack Seward cabled me, I knew of the vampire. But as I said this morning, we don't jump to that conclusion."

They were quiet a moment, the fiddle filling the air.

Then it was Abraham's turn to ask Brigid how she came to know of the vampire in the lodge.

Her face flushed and she told him, "I don't think you'd believe me."

He assumed she was an amateur *monster hunter*, seeking him out for advice. *In that, she must be disappointed.* "Tell me anyway."

"I'll need to show you something for you to understand." She rose hesitantly from the table and beckoned him. The nearby tables were empty as she walked past them. "It has to do with how you described the nature of the vampire. I was curious about it after encountering that one at the lodge. I've always been interested in weird history, and one day I hiked to Montpelier to see for myself. We all grew up with the stories. Instead, I found that thing, rabid then as it was today."

Its ferocity burning in his memory, he was astounded. "You were lucky to have gotten away."

She stopped after the third table at an opening where, on the wall, was a decorated mirror, painted with a brewery's name. She took his hand and pulled him closer.

"I didn't," she said. "Just bad luck I scratched it and its blood dripped in my mouth…"

Van Helsing gasped and his knees buckled. *He saw only himself in the mirror.* He made to pull away and put as much distance between them as he could.

"Please don't be afraid, and please don't run," she pleaded, desperation in her eyes. "I'm not here to harm you. I want your help."

He had instinctually begun to raise his rosary from his pocket, and when Brigid noticed this, she reacted not with fear but with sadness. There was profound sorrow written on her face, a forlorn look of someone who felt truly alone. This and the fact that she didn't shy away from the cross inspired him to conceal it again. She asked him to please sit and just speak with her a bit, and against his initial judgement, he acquiesced.

"You don't retreat from the cross," he observed as they took their seats. "How is that?"

"I love the cross. I'm Catholic, just like me parents raised me." She took a drink and continued sadly. "It just doesn't like me anymore."

"Would it burn you to touch it?"

"Aye. I tried to put on a Celtic cross necklace my gran gave me and couldn't get the smell of me own burning skin out of my nose for days."

The old man was astounded. A vampire who could stand the presence of a crucifix. He'd never heard of it! He thought of the many other theories he could test. If one aspect of the lore proved untrue on this girl, what else could she disprove? The possibilities for experimentation…He caught Brigid's eyes and the emotion he saw there reminded him that she was a person. He'd just thought of her as a test subject, a vampire only, ignoring that for all appearances, the girl across from him still seemed to have a soul. He remembered Miss Lucy, the Transylvanian and his brides, none he had encountered seemed to have a shred of humanity left, none of his research alluded to the possibility. Remarkably, Brigid made him drop his guard. "You want my help, you say?"

"I need you to tell me any ways you know to break this curse." Her hands clasped in front of her, pleading with him, and he felt an urge to reach over and take them.

"My child, the only way I know is to kill the one who turned you…" He remembered Mina and how she had come back from the brink. But she had not turned completely, and he knew why this would bring Brigid little comfort.

A lone tear slithered down her cheek, which she swiped away nonchalantly. "Yes, I knew that one, too. S'why I hoped to bring you to the hill. So, we've done that, and I'm unchanged." She prayed, "Nothing else?"

He felt his own sadness well up at her desperation. "I'm sorry, my dear. I've never encountered tell of another way."

She took a deep sip of her pint, breathed deeply, and looked at him with a stony resolve. "Then the next thing I beg your help with is this: I need you to kill me."

Abraham shook at the request and jolted back in his seat. "*Mein Gott!*" he coughed. "Why would you make such a request?"

"You said it yourself this morning. As a vampire, my nature is inherently evil. I haven't tasted human blood since the night I turned, but it's only a matter of time before I can't control myself. I am, as you said, a soulless afront to the Lord, incapable of living a civilized life, always bound by my thirst." There was no malice in her voice, but she was pointed. "If this is my future, I don't want it."

Van Helsing considered, his mind a maelstrom of possibilities. "But, my child, you are the most civilized I have known a vampire to be. I was speaking from my own experience. You certainly don't fit my experience." She softened a little. "You say you haven't tasted human blood since you turned. How, then, have you survived?"

"I've gotten blood from a butcher's shop when I can, when I feel I need it. And there have been a few unfortunate animals."

"There, then, you can sustain yourself without taking life—at least human life!"

"I don't want to take animal life, either! I didn't even eat meat before!"

"The butcher, then. I'm sure we can find you an arrangement with one or two…"

"Don't act as though you weren't prepared to kill me moments ago. You could do it then, you can do it now." Brigid seemed almost angry that he was evading her request.

"That was gut instinct. You must, again, remember, I have only encountered murderous vampires. You are undoing much of my notion of what I know." He paused. "You have found a way to survive without taking life, why do you want to die so badly?"

The stony resolve broke, and the dam of tears burst. "The night I turned," she sobbed. "I killed me parents." Her voice cracked as she spoke. "I still see their horrified faces, every time I close my eyes. I didn't know how to control it; I woke up and had this insatiable hunger. I could *hear* their pulses and I just pounced!" She was shaking now, the weight of her actions racking her with guilt. "I *never* want that to happen again."

Van Helsing moved to her side of the booth and took her hands to console her. He too was shaken, everything he thought he knew all these years about vampires crashing down, decades of research quashed in one night. But here was opportunity, too. To learn and to grow. "My dear child," he said softly, "you need to know that was not your nature. That was a force beyond your understanding trying to take root. But you fought it off. Later than you'd like, and I'm terribly sorry about your parents—but you did fight it off. That takes incredible strength. And the remorse you feel? *That* is your nature. That is how you can know you will never let it happen again."

He raised her face to look at him. "I am not going to grant your request. But I promise I will do my utmost to help you. We will learn how you get through life like this and we will explore alternative ways to break the curse together. I promise, you are not alone."

Brigid, still crying, smiled slightly and softened again. "I don't understand. The way you spoke before, why would you help me like that?"

Van Helsing laughed. "Child, did you listen to my lecture? I am a scientist! And a good scientist must be willing to keep an open mind when presented with new information. God forgives, I learn."

The vampire and the monster hunter talked long into the night—and for many nights thereafter—sharing ideas to shake the certainty of science, religion, and superstition.

Bill Cozza has always drifted to dark literature, and was inspired to start writing after reading *Dracula* at a young age, the start of a lifelong passion for horror. He is a member of the HWA, and his story "Reclamation" was published in Issue 7 of *Dracula Beyond Stoker*. When not writing, Bill works in the tech industry, and he spends his time watching horror films, reading comic books, or from a never-ending pile of novels. He lives in Media, Pennsylvania with his wife and daughter, and their cats.

Smoke and Mirrors
By Mark Oxbrow

VAN HELSING. *(TO AUDIENCE)* Just a moment, Ladies and Gentlemen! Just a word before you go. We hope the memories of Dracula…won't give you bad dreams…When you get home tonight and the lights have been turned out and you are afraid to look behind the curtains and you dread to see a face appear at the window…why, just pull yourself together and remember that after all *there are such things.*
(Curtain falls.)
—Dracula, *The Vampire Play,* 1927
Hamilton Deane & Jean Balderston

Letter to Professor Abraham Van Helsing

Wien IX
Berggasse 19
Vienna
Austria

9 September 1927

Dear colleague,

I am indebted to you for so kindly sending me Harenberg's *Vernünftige und Christliche Gedancken über die Vampirs*. Such a rare and extraordinary book.

You may know of my abiding fascination with the occult and paranormal. Not quite an obsession, but much more than idle curiosity.

I have made no secret of my interest, presenting two papers 'The Uncanny' and 'Psychoanalysis and Telepathy' to the Central Committee of the International Psychoanalytical Association. In recent years, I have made a close study of prophetic dreams and thought transmission.

I will not dismiss the study of so-called occult psychic phenomena as unscientific. If I were at the beginning rather than at the end of my scientific career, as I am today, I might pursue just this field of research, in spite of all difficulties.

But the belief that the dead may walk and gorge on the blood of the living? I fear I am utterly incapable of considering the 'vampire' as a scientific possibility.

That said, as an occult scholar, I barely qualify as a novice, with no right to claim so much as a hint of authority. And so it is, professor, that I humbly seek your expertise.

I have a patient—a young lady, newly returned from England—and I believe that your insight in her case may prove indispensable.

She was discovered, wandering lost in Vienna, picking roses in the Volksgarten. Her hands torn bloody by thorns.

There was nothing to identify her save a receipt from the tearooms of J. Lyons and Co. of Piccadilly, London, with the owords 'Elodie 9/6' on the reverse. Perhaps 9 shillings and sixpence?

'Elodie' is convinced that vampires attack her, feeding on her.

She fears that she will die, and wake in her grave, un-dead, a vampire.

I pray you will come to Vienna.

Dr. Sigmund Freud

Professor Abraham Van Helsing's Journal
(Translated from Dutch)

Amsterdam, Friday 9 September 1927.—I saw them once more, this morning, a little after first light.

The three vampires are just as dear Mina and Jonathan describe: a widow, dressed all in black, veiled, hidden beneath a shroud. She walks with her daughter, pushing a baby carriage.

She mirrors my footsteps, always there, crossing the Prinsengracht canal, close as my shadow. Never falling far behind.

I know the widow's name. Ana Florescu. Vampire.

She is the daughter of Sofia Lazarescu. I cut her mother's head from her body at Castle Dracula. Her gold hair curled about my fingers as I took a knife to her throat. Dracula's three vampire brides, slumbering soundly in their tombs. I hammered rowan stakes through their hearts and took their heads.

Ana haunts me now.

The widow walks with her child at her side. Sofia Luminita Florescu. Seven years old when Dracula took her life. Mina tells me that Sofia will take the form of a monstrous wolf with black fur.

I do not know the baby's name. She is Ana's sister, torn, undead, from Lazarescu's womb. Never to be baptised. Unchristened, nameless, Godforsaken. Sleeping by day in graveyard earth. Swaddled at night in her baby carriage. No milk to comfort her cries. Nothing to sup but blood.

God help her.

Saturday 10 September.—I saw them. The three accursed weird sisters. Damned creatures. They stand on the Papiermolensluis bridge over the canal, watching me at my windows.

Later.—There came a knock on my door, a little after nine this night.

I wore a sprig of wolfsbane, queen of poisons, in my lapel and kept a Sacred Wafer in my hand.

It was the daughter, Sofia. So small. Never aging beyond her seven years. Her face hidden beneath a black veil.

She held out a letter.

Letter from Ana Florescu to Van Helsing

Van Helsing,

I sorrow to see that you have been unwell.

You have become so aged and frail. Your hair silvering, back bending. Your fingers crooked, eyes losing the light. I fear for you.

Can you see to read your books? Does the candlelight dim, colours fade to naught?

Do not die, my dear Van Helsing. I have such beautiful things to show you before you die.

All these years I have fed on the misery of your dearest friends. Did you know? Did you guess you were to blame for their ill fortune?

Poor Arthur Holmwood, a lord with no heirs. No sons to carry his noble name. To lose his wife so young, her belly fat with child. Blood and brains dashed out in the snow. Such a pity. He never thought he would find love again, not after Lucy.

Did you hear he is married once more? Married out of duty but always he had such a soft heart. And children tumbling out. Beautiful boys, soft girls. Tiny purple fingers, lungs drowning in blood and pus. All his pretty ones dead. So many little graves all in a row. His children rotting in the earth and his poor wife lost her wits.

Doctor John Seward. So kindly. Your dear friend of so many years. He took Arthur's wife for him, locked her up safe in Bedlam. She claws at her face. Did you see? Deep bloody wounds and ragged scars. And never a sound from her lips.

And whatever did become of Doctor Seward's beloved wife? Such a pale, frightened thing. Do you hear what it is they say? That she shared his taste for morphine? Missing is such an ugly word. Maybe she lives, lost in her delirium, intoxicated, selling herself for opium?

Jonathan and Mina Harker. Did you not love them most? I think you did. They barely need my help to sow and reap their suffering. A daughter dead. Another lost, so far from home, to books and medicine. And their son, Quincey?

I came to Harker's son, out there, in No-Man's Land, at the Battle of Mons. Bloody and cowering in mud and gore. I thought to tear his throat out, to devour him. But he wanted to die.

The others prayed. Child, wife, beloved friend, no matter— all died fearful and begging to be spared. But Quincey Harker smiled and gave me thanks, so I left him in agony.

I had all eternity to wait. To watch him heal, his torment fading. I was there, watching, at his wedding. I saw you, Van Helsing, wishing him and his bride well. And his baby, Mina and Jonathan's granddaughter, Séraphine. I waited for her to heal their failing hearts, and I fed her with my blood.

They think they have saved her. Cured her. But she will grow, and fade and die and rise once more un-dead. This you know, Van Helsing. You must destroy me to save poor Séraphine.

But it is too late. You are so weak, undone. Age has withered you. What strength you once had is lost. You feel it all fading. What were their names? I see you write in your journals, trying to capture your days before you forget.

You will lose everything you love before you die.

Ana Florescu

Professor Abraham Van Helsing's Journal

Tuesday 13 September.—I keep the windows shuttered and barred, garlic flowers above my door.

There is a loaded revolver on the nightstand and my golok—a heavy Javanese blade—is never far from my hand.

I have not seen the three vampires, but I feel they are close.

This morning, I received a letter from Doctor Sigmund Freud.

He bids me come to Vienna, to consult with him on an urgent case.

I will settle my affairs and leave tomorrow.

Thursday 15 September.—The journey from Amsterdam to Vienna was tolerable. Inevitably, the train was delayed, and I narrowly avoided missing the express at Basel.

I find it impossible to sleep on trains.

My bones are become a curse. Arthritis, rheumatism, osseous atrophy. Aspirin proved useless. I took a tincture of laudanum with brandy. Some small relief from the unrelenting pain.

Later.—Met at 19 Berggasse by Miss Anna Freud.

She showed much concern for my ills. Her father was resting. She made me *Schwarzer Kaffee*—black coffee. The coffee at Café Karpershoek is more to my liking.

Doctor Freud is a remarkable soul. He is never without a cigar, offering me Reina Cubanas, asking if I smoke Liliputanos.

His daughter Anna wrote in shorthand, scribbling relentlessly, as we spoke.

Anna Freud's notes—Professor Van Helsing & Dr Sigmund Freud

Thursday 15 September 1927 at Berggasse 19

Freud: I hope you can help me, Professor. Vampirism, I seek to define it precisely—what it is, and, crucially, what it is not. How do you define the vampire?

Van Helsing: I bow to Johann Heinrich Zopfius, in his *Dissertatio de Vampiris Serviensibus*, "Vampires are spectres of the dead that come forth from their graves at night, attacking men, women, and children as they sleep quiet in their beds, sparing neither age nor sex, sucking out the blood from their bodies, destroying them utterly."

Freud: And that belief has its origins in the Balkans?

Van Helsing: Yes. Zopfius writes in 1733 of vampires appearing in Serbia, in the village of Medvedia. There was an Austrian army doctor, named Johann Flückinger. He documented the case of Arnont Paule, a vampire. More than a dozen villagers died.

Freud: Yes, I have read the reports written by Flückinger and Glaser.

Van Helsing: These two were military men, disciplined, rigorous. Surgeons trained in Vienna, this very city, sent to the edge of the Habsburg empire. They saw the bodies of the dead, exhumed vampires from their graves. Corpses uncorrupted, nails and hair newly grown, fresh blood about their mouths, a glut of blood in their stomachs.

Freud: The tales these men were told—doubtless these were nothing but superstitions. Some dark arcane magic that science seeks to illuminate. Beliefs founded on irrational fears. We fear death—so is it not natural to fear that the dead, the un-dead, will walk and take us with them, down into the grave?

Van Helsing: I believe they reported the truth.

Freud: Superstitions have power. Would you agree? I believed in the significance of numbers. Numbers in Pythagorean mysticism. The Gematria of the Kabbalah. In 1899, my telephone number was 14362 and I believed, I was utterly convinced…that those last two digits foretold the age I would die—sixty-two.

Van Helsing: And how old are you now?

Freud: Seventy-one. This fear was not rational, but it overwhelmed me. Tell me, professor, what do you know of Empress Maria Theresa?

Van Helsing: She was ruler of the Hapsburg empire. Austria, Hungary, Bohemia, Transylvania…I believe her palace is quite near?

Freud: Schönbrunn Palace. It is perhaps a little less than five miles. Did you know that Empress Maria Theresa sent her personal physician, Gerard van Swieten, to investigate the vampire panic?

Van Helsing: I did.

Freud: He found nothing but fear and superstitious credulity. He believed the cause was the simplicity and ignorance of the peasantry…

Van Helsing: The Empress's physician. Born, raised and educated in enlightened Vienna. It was impossible for him to believe anything else. His reputation would not have survived any other diagnosis. Fear. Ignorance. The courtly always refuse to believe or learn from the poor.

Freud: I believe that psychiatry can divine the truth of vampirism. As with the lunatic, the insanity of the werewolf is laid bare. Lunacy—lunaticus—affected by the moon. So it is with the vampire. A sadistic compulsion, the desire to drink blood, to cut and bite and hurt, to kill…

Van Helsing: Do you deny that evil exists?

Freud: Evil? There is a fascination with transgression, the breaking of taboos. To defy God and break the Covenant. The vampire pursues self-gratification, without conscience, committing violent acts of murder and necrophagia—eating the flesh of the human dead.

Van Helsing: So, doctor, it is your belief that vampires are merely human?

Freud: Richard von Krafft-Ebing, a German psychiatrist defined vampirism as Psychopathia Sexualis. You will have read Krafft-Ebing? He recounts the case of a 19-year-old vinedresser named Leger. After days wandering a forest, he murders a 12-year-old girl. He mutilates her body, tears out her heart and drinks her blood.

Van Helsing: Albin Grau, a student of my friend, Professor Arminius Vámbéry, of Buda-Pesth University, had cause to visit Dimitrescu, an isolated village in the Carpathians. Grau was taken by a young woman, named Ana Florescau, to the ruins of a medieval castle, high in the mountains.

He saw the tombs of three vampire women—vampires that I beheaded. Grau never returned from Castle Dracula. Ana Florescau broke his bones. Her daughter Sofia and infant sister fed on his blood and flesh. Lately, I have seen these three weird sisters walking in Amsterdam. None have aged a day.

Freud: You have witnessed these things, first hand?

Van Helsing: Yes, I have. Twenty years ago, I would vehemently argue, showing you evidence, proof that vampires are real. I no longer feel the need to quarrel. You will believe—or not. I am too old and too tired to care. Doctor, you may count these creatures among the living, but they are vampires. They are un-dead.

Freud: Professor, to the case of the young woman. Her name is Elodie. 17-years old. She is a neurasthenic, pitifully tortured. She barely sleeps, craving light, with a dreadful, overwhelming fear of the dark…

Van Helsing: Go on.

Freud: Elodie is not feeble minded. She appears afflicted with hebephrenia—her speech and behaviour disordered. She laughs inappropriately at the most distressing news. Her mannerisms are odd, her decision-making poor. She believes that vampires bit her throat, sucking her blood.

Van Helsing: Does Elodie suffer from melancholia, hysterical delusions?

Freud: Yes…but…

Van Helsing: Johann Wier wrote that the melancholic are particularly vulnerable to the devil and his infernal kin. *De Praestigiis Daemonum*, 1563. The vampire chooses its victims with care, preying, like the ravenous wolf, upon the weak. Doctor, you must take me to Elodie. Her life, her very soul is in danger.

Professor Abraham Van Helsing's Journal

Thursday 15 September.—Doctor Freud describes Elodie as suffering from 'morbid dread.' He believes that deep, within her subconscious is a desire to be possessed, to be at the mercy of another. He tells me it is her fear of this loss of control that terrifies her, that haunts her sleeping mind.

Elodie has wounds upon her neck, shoulders and arms. 'Lesions' the doctor calls them. He says that these injuries are self-inflicted, that Elodie has torn at her own flesh with a hatpin or brooch, stabbed at her skin with sharp scissors.

She is not believed. The doctors she has turned to for help, for her very salvation, think she suffers from delusions. They write in their notes that she cuts herself, that her thoughts are disorganised, that her fears are irrational.

Elodie is 17 years old. A child. Her skin is pale as ivory. God protect her. Watch over her. Keep her from harm.

There are spots of blood on her nightdress. She sits, barefoot. Her knees drawn up to her body, her spine curved as she makes herself small. She hides her face behind her dark hair. It falls, loose about her shoulders. She twirls strands around her fingers as she speaks.

Anna kindly scribed our words.

Anna Freud's notes—Professor Van Helsing & Elodie

Thursday 15 September 1927

Van Helsing: Elodie, my name is Abraham Van Helsing. I am a professor. I want you to know that I will do all I can to keep you safe.

Elodie: (singing) *Come dame or maid, be not afraid.... dame or maid.*

Van Helsing: Elodie, will you tell me why you were in England?

Elodie: (singing) *I see…I see the stars at bloody wars.*

Van Helsing: Doctor Freud tells me that you are a parlour-maid.

Elodie: (singing) *Parlourmaid, a parlourmaid, be not afraid. I gots the keys. Jingling and jangling. And bells at the door. Good morrow, will you wait in the drawing room? If you'd be so kind. The mistress will be down presently.*

Van Helsing: Who was your mistress, Elodie?

Elodie: A fine lady. Fine. Rings on her fingers, bells on her toes. Round the hollow tree. The Queen of the Woods.

Van Helsing: And you were her parlourmaid?

Elodie: No. Dame or maid. Scrub the hearth. Shovel coal. Set the fires. Did you see the chimney sweeps, dancing on May morning? Round the May Poles. Pretty flowers in my hair. Pretty.

Van Helsing: Did someone come to the house? Maybe to visit your mistress?

Elodie: Dressed in black. Dressed in black. Silver buttons down her back.

Van Helsing: A lady? Dressed in black? Was she with some-one? Elodie?

Elodie: Girl?

Van Helsing: Girl? Did you see a lady dress in black? And a girl?

Elodie: Sofia.

Van Helsing: What?

Elodie: Poor little things—lay down and died. And when they were dead. Sofia is dead. Sofia. Sofia is dead. The Robins so red. Brought strawberry leaves. Blood on my dress.

Van Helsing: Blood?

Elodie: Sofia and her mother, out in the woods. Out by the hollow tree. And baby makes three.

Van Helsing: There was a baby?

Elodie: Lady Bird, Lady Bird. Fly away home.

Van Helsing: Elodie. You saw a baby?

Elodie: Out in the woods. I met a girl. I cut her throat. I sucked her blood. And left her skin a hanging-o.

Van Helsing: Elodie. Was it Sofia or the lady dressed in black? Did Sofia cut your throat?

Elodie: A cat came fiddling out of a barn. With a pair of bag-pipes under her arm. She could sing nothing but fiddle de dee. The mouse has married the bumble-bee. Pipe, cat,—dance, mouse. We'll have a wedding at Hillingham House.

Van Helsing: What? Elodie…what did you say? Hillingham?

Elodie: When good king Arthur ruled this land. He was a goodly king.

Van Helsing: Arthur? Arthur Holmwood, was your mistress Lady Godalming?

Elodie: Lady Bird, Lady Bird. Fly away home. Your house is on fire. Your children will burn.

Van Helsing: Elodie. You have done so well. Be not afraid.

Professor Abraham Van Helsing's Journal

Friday 16 September.—Doctor Freud's patient, the young girl, Elodie. I pray God will protect her.

I have left detailed instructions. Crucifixes for her rooms and wreaths of garlic. The doctor is treating her with transfusions of blood.

It seems that Elodie was the maid of Arthur Holmwood. It was Arthur that inherited Hillingham House after the death of his fiancé, dear Miss Lucy Westenra.

Lord and Lady Godalming.

The three vampires that killed Arthur's wife and children, tortured this poor girl. They fed on her. Mutilated her. Doctor Freud tells me she was found wandering in Vienna, anaemic, near death from loss of blood.

She was taken from London to satiate their thirst, as their plaything on their travels. God preserve her.

I took my leave of Doctor Freud and his daughter, catching the Orient Express. The doctor gave me a Reina Cubana, and three Austrian Trabucco cigars.

I have not ridden this train for thirty years. I sat in its carriages with John Seward, drinking brandy. Sleep would not come. Dracula and his brides were gone, but we lost Quincey Morris, his coffin in the baggage car. Arthur Holmwood refused to abandon his vigil. Jonathan and Mina Harker never left their compartment.

Vienna. Munich. Strasbourg. Paris Gare de l'Est. Calais.

I telephoned John Seward from Vienna. He will expect me in London. Seward is calling on Arthur, and telephoning Mina and Jonathan to join us from Paris.

Thirty years. We faced Dracula, together.

Doctor John Seward's Diary

Bethlem Royal Hospital, St. George's Fields, Southwark, London
Saturday 17 September.—Van Helsing arrives this afternoon, at London Victoria. Jonathan and Mina will be arriving on Monday. Jonathan did not sound well.

I called on Arthur this afternoon, at Hillingham. The staff have not seen hide nor hair of him for a fortnight. He is not to be found at the Godalming estate in Ring, at the Albemarle Hotel, or in any of his usual haunts.

Later.—*I* met Van Helsing at Victoria. We took the Circle Line, changing at Embankment for the Northern Line. He has a room at the Queen's Hotel in Leicester Square, so we took a table for dinner at the Garrick Club.

Unexpectedly, the Garrick's Hall Porter handed me a letter.

Letter to Doctor John Seward from Arthur Holmwood,
Lord Godalming

7 Sept.

Jack

My sincere apologies. I hope you will forgive my sudden absence.

I confide in you Jack, counting in your discretion.

It is a rather delicate matter.

You will recall our night at the Little Theatre in March? I much prefer Dracula portrayed on stage than in the flesh.

I doubt you will recollect the young actress that played the Housemaid in your Asylum? Her name is Miss Eleanor Fernley, understudy to both Betty Murgatroyd and Kilda Macleod.

I fear I have become a cliché. The English lord that falls in love with an actress. But nevertheless, I am besotted.

Miss Fernley is joining some of the English cast of Dracula for the play's run in New Haven, Hartford, et al before New York.

She has asked me to join her in America and I have accepted.

A hack from the Illustrated London News is sniffing around the West End, and, to quote the Bard—'the better part of valour is discretion.'

You can imagine the scandal. Somewhere between the Duke of Clarence's indiscretions at Cleveland Street and Bertie's affair with Lily Langtry.

Please do take care of Rosalind.

Art H.

Doctor John Seward's Diary

Saturday 17 September.—I kept Arthur's letter from Van Helsing, simply telling him that Art is travelling in the United States.

It will be two years, come December, that Art's wife, Rosalind, has been in my care at Bethlem. There is no improvement in her condition. To bury all your children.

I sometimes think it is a blessing that Charlotte and I remained childless.

Letter to Lucy Harker from Mina Harker

London. Monday 19 September

My dearest Lucy,

London is dreary. Paris was warm and golden as we departed. England's skies are dark and rainy. I hope you have blue sky and sunshine in Edinburgh.

Do you recall Dr John Seward? He has a promotion: principal physician at Bethlem Royal Hospital, Southwark. Our dear friend Professor Abraham Van Helsing is visiting from the Netherlands. He had hoped to see Lord Godalming, but it seems that Arthur has sailed to the United States.

You danced at Arthur's wedding when you were a child, standing on your father's toes as he whirled you around. Sadly, Arthur's wife, Rosalind, is a patient under John Seward's care. We visited her this afternoon. She did not know us, never raising her eyes. John spoke of melancholia. She has not spoken a word in years.

It is nearly six years since the disappearance of John Seward's wife, Charlotte.

She was radiant. She doted on you when you were a babe, and on your brother Quincey too. Charlotte would buy you both chocolate éclairs, delighting in the mess you made!

I will never believe that Charlotte simply abandoned John. She loved him deeply. John smiles as we speak of her, but he cannot hide his sorrow. He has never recovered from her loss.

All my love.

Professor Abraham Van Helsing's Journal

Tuesday 20 September.—It is not possible.

'Everything you love.' The vampire, Ana Florescu's words, 'You will lose everything you love before you die.'

We breakfasted together at the Hotel Metropole. Mina and Jonathan were in fine spirits, talking about Quincey, their daughter-in-law Élise and their granddaughter Séraphine. John Seward had to depart early, attending to his duties at Bethlem Asylum.

Thirty years ago we four stood against Dracula.

I swear I saw the three vampires on the Strand. Across the street, passing by St Dunstan-in-the-West, dressed in black as Elodie said.

We were to meet my dear friend John later that afternoon in his quarters. There was a delivery waiting for him. A hat box.

Inside was Charlotte's head.

Her dead eyes stared out, her lips sewn shut. They tore her head from her body. The hat box was full of playbills, pamphlets advertising a theatre show:

'Dracula—The Vampire Play

Fulton Theatre. 46th Street, West of Broadway, New York City

Matinees Wednesday and Saturday

Dramatized by Hamilton Deane and John Balderston from Bram Stoker's Famous Novel "Dracula"

Synopsis of Scenes

Act I

Library in Dr. Seward's Sanitorium at Purley. Evening.

Act II

Lucy's Boudoir. Evening of the Following Day.

Act III

Scene 1—same as Act I. Thirty-two hours later.

Scene 2—A Vault. Just after Sunrise.'

Wednesday 21 September.—Last night, a little after midnight, my beloved friend Doctor John Seward died.

We sat with him, in his library, as night fell. He injected morphine, not caring that I saw the needle marks scarring his arms. I refused to let him out of my sight for a moment.

He paced the room, trying to make sense of the horrors we saw. Did the vampires keep Charlotte alive these past six years? John tells us that the playbills are a threat, that Arthur is in New York with an actress, Miss Eleanor Fernley, an understudy cast in the Dracula play.

I thought John was pouring a drink. He carried a bottle of gin in his hand. I did not see the revolver till he raised it to his temple.

Eternal Father, I offer Thee the Most Precious Blood of Thy Divine Son, Jesus, in union with the Masses said throughout the world today, for all the Holy Souls in Purgatory, for sinners everywhere.

Mina Harker's Journal

RMS Olympic, White Star Line, Thursday 29 September.— Professor Van Helsing has barely spoken a word since Bethlem. I think he blames himself for John's death.

Jonathan stalks our cabin, circling, refusing to set foot out on the deck. I saw his anger as we hunted Dracula, but this is worse. This rage consumes him.

We arrive in New York in one week. I pray we find Arthur in time.

Professor Abraham Van Helsing's Journal

New York City, Friday 7 October.—It has come to this.

We found Arthur Holmwood at the Fulton Theatre. Opening night was Wednesday. Tonight, we take our seats for Dracula, not knowing what Ana Florescu intends.

I fear that John Seward was right: the playbills in the hat box are a warning, a threat to Arthur and Miss Eleanor. The three vampires, these weird sisters, lay a trap for us.

The theatre will be our field of battle.

Arthur secured us a tour of the stage. Mina recalled a tour of the Lyceum Theatre in London, led by Bram Stoker. He showed her the secrets of the stage. The gaslights, scenery and rigging, the trapdoors. She recalled the 'grave trap' and the 'vampire trap.'

This 'vampire trap' was famed at the Lyceum, as the 'Corsican Trap' was particular to the Gaiety Theatre. It was constructed by a James R. Planché for his play 'The Brides of the Isles.' The vampire Lord Ruthven disappeared and made his entrance by means of this trapdoor cut in the stage.

Dracula at the Fulton has its own 'vampire trap.' Smoke and mirrors.

The actor portraying Dracula is a Hungarian, classically trained in Buda-Pesth. His name is Bela Lugosi. Mister Lugosi was kind enough to show us his playscript and walk us through the theatrical effect that the vampire trap conjures.

'(DRACULA, with loud burst of mocking laughing, goes down vampire trap on the word "sun," leaving the TWO MEN holding the empty cape. As soon as they've seen trap back in place, HARKER backs down L., drops empty cape in front of desk, then a FLASH goes off in front of fireplace. The THREE MEN look around them.) (WARN Curtain and BLACKOUT.)'

We are determined to set a trap for Ana Florescu and her daughter Sofia. The vampires have set the battleground. Here we will face them.

Saturday 8 October.—Jonathan told me it was an odd thing to see his life depicted by another in Nosferatu. I had not imagined it. To see an actor, this Edward Van Sloan, play me, and trade words with Mister Lugosi. This Dracula is so far from the abomination we faced. Dracula attired in evening dress with shined shoes and a cape. Bizarre.

Tonight's show was uneventful. After, out on 7th Avenue, I thought I saw the widow and her child. I pray I was mistaken.

Wednesday 12 October.—Miss Eleanor Fernley took to the stage this evening. Ms. Nedda Harrigan was taken unwell, so Miss Fernley plays the Maid.

There is blood on these pages.

In Act II, Dracula leans close, saying, "In the past five hundred years, Professor, those who have crossed my path have all died…"

At that moment a shape appeared on stage, emerging from the wings.

A black wolf. Monstrous. Eyes red, fangs bared. And there, in the shadows, was the vampire, Ana Florescu, her veil drawn back. Blood smeared across her face.

In her left hand she held a human jaw.

The audience faltered, not knowing if this were part of the play. A split second later the theatre was in uproar—screaming, panic—all tearing from their seats as the wolf padded out across the stage.

Never have I seen such sights.

I fought my way against the tide, battling to make it backstage from the stalls.

Jonathan was cursing, taking aim and firing his Webley Revolver. The wolf turned to face him, snarling, bounding across the stage, leaping down upon him.

I could not stop to worry at Harker's fate. I pushed on, breaking through the terrified crowds.

There was Ana, at the edge of the spotlight, and Mister Lugosi playing his part.

"You fools!" Lugosi raged, "You think you can destroy me?"

For a moment Ana was distracted, her attention drawn to Dracula in his cape. In that instant our trap was sprung.

On cue, Arthur Holmwood, knife in hand, appeared from the vampire trap, out from under the stage.

I hoped this sleight of hand might give Arthur the precious time he needed. He lunged forward, the knife raised, but Ana was not fooled.

The blade stabbed through her palm, jutting out the back of her right hand. She did not flinch. A smile cut across her face as she thrust the jawbone into Arthur's carotid artery.

Bone and tooth sliced his flesh, tearing open his neck. Arthur staggered, drowning in his blood.

The wolf fell on Jonathan, I saw it now from the footlights. Claws tore at his face, fangs ripping. And there was Mina, throwing herself upon the wolf's back, stabbing at the creature with a bayonet.

I would have fallen then, if not for Mina. I heard her screams —not fear, but fury.

The Colt Service Revolver in my hand fired. I wonder still, did my eyesight fail me or was Ana too quick? The bullet caught her hair but cracked a hole in Arthur's forehead, piercing his skull.

She was upon me before I drew breath. Bloody hands on my face, bones breaking in my wrist. The gun fell as I collapsed to my knees. Ana. So fair. Her lips red, skin as white as new fallen snow.

Her teeth bit into my throat. I felt the breath drawn into my lungs. So many years since I had felt such bliss, intoxicating, seething through my veins.

Mina was screaming. It did not matter. She was nothing.

I knelt, delirious, euphoric. Spellbound. I gave myself utterly to Ana.

Something moved, a formless shape seen out the corner of my eye. A vampire cape. The actor, Bela Lugosi, storming across the stage, Dracula, Arthur's knife held in his fist.

I wanted to cry out, to warn Ana of the danger, but I faltered. She eased an inch away, licking her lips. I was a broken thing, spine crooked, blood spilling from my throat. Pain gnawing at my old bones.

Lugosi jammed the knife into Ana's side. It slid between two of her ribs, piercing her heart. She shuddered, back arching.

I took hold of the knife as Lugosi staggered back, dragging it out of the wound.

Ana shrieked, digging her fingernails into my flesh as I lashed out. The knife cut deep into her neck. I stabbed once more, severing her jugular. I felt the blade scrape against her spine.

She was falling, bowing her back. I was relentless. Hacking at her throat, the knife cutting through flesh and sinew, carving through bone. Her body spasmed as I severed her head. It lay there, on the stage, dead eyes staring up into the spotlight.

There came a dreadful baying from the wolf, howling, keening. It tore itself away from the Harkers, stumbling out into the aisle. A mess of bloody wounds and tangled fur. It loped away. Sofia, claws ripping at the seats, bounding over the stalls. Leaving her mother's corpse behind.

Monday 24 October, Paris, France.—The body of Arthur Holmwood has been laid to rest at Highgate Cemetery, in the tomb of Lucy Westenra.

Miss Eleanor is well provided for in his will, but no fortune will ease her mourning. She lost her love that night in New York. If Ms. Harrigan had not fallen ill, and Eleanor not taken to the stage, she may have lost her life.

It is a joy to see Quincey, Élise and their daughter Séraphine. Jonathan's wounds are healing, tended by his beloved Mina.

Séraphine and Elodie are delivered from the vampire. God keep them safe.

And so, the curtain falls.

I saw them by the river this morning. A seven-year-old child, Sofia, dressed in black, pushing a baby carriage. I hope that somehow they too will find peace.

Mark Oxbrow is a storyteller, author and ghostwriter. His short story, 'White as Snow, Red as Blood' was published by *Dracula Beyond Stoker*, accompanying Issue One. His story 'Frightful Things' published in *Dracula Beyond Stoker Issue 3: The Bloofer Lady*, was recommended by legendary editor Ellen Datlow as one of the best horror short stories of the year. Mark's books feature ghost stories, witch goddesses, Arthurian legends, poison gardens, folk horror, medieval monsters and secret treasures. Mark was born and raised in Edinburgh, the world's most haunted city. Over twenty-five years ago, he founded Scotland's largest Halloween festival.

Strange Bedfellows
By Henry Herz

8:20 a.m., October 9 – Freer, TX

A shiny white Chevy G-series van with Amigo Energy logos on its sides rolled along rural Magnolia Road. In it sat four vampire hunters.

From the passenger seat, thirty-year-old Quincey Van Helsing tapped the driver's right arm. "We just passed the target's driveway, Ted."

The six-foot-tall, bushy-bearded driver nodded and eased the van onto the dirt shoulder.

Van Helsing turned backward, drawing a squeak from the leatherette seat. "How are things looking, Chelsea?"

Staring at her laptop through black-rimmed glasses, the slender woman smiled. "The surveillance camera's working great. The target's just sitting on his couch looking at his phone."

"Perfect." Quincey's eyes shifted to the mocha-skinned, NFL lineman-sized fourth member of the team. "Samir will breach the front door, then we'll force the target into a corner so I can *convince* him to tell us who made him. Let's go."

The four slipped out of the van. They wore matching black work boots, blue-gray pants, baseball caps, and zipped-up blue-gray softshell jackets with Amigo Energy patches on the right breast.

Concealed beneath their jackets, silver crucifixes hung on long chains. Leather dual-shoulder holsters held Smith & Wesson Model 500 .50-caliber five-shot revolvers with 7.5-inch-long barrels. Two foot-long sharpened wooden stakes also hung from the holsters. Van Helsing led them across the road briskly but quietly. Samir lugged a red, twenty-inch metal toolbox which, like the revolvers, wasn't Amigo Energy standard issue. It contained no tools and had two extra handles rotated perpendicular to its length. The prior day, it had been partially filled with molten tin. At sixty-five pounds, the toolbox had more than twice the weight of door-breaching battering rams used by police.

Reaching the front door of the ochre Mid-Century Modern home, Quincey gave Samir a subtle nod. All four of them unzipped their jackets.

Grasping the toolbox by both handles, Samir pivoted his upper torso. With a grunt, he swung the toolbox full force into the door, just above the lock. The frame shattered and the door slammed inward.

Samir dropped the toolbox with a thud, and the four charged inside. Each drew a wooden stake with their right hand and brandished a crucifix in their left.

Taken completely by surprise, the target, a blond-haired man in his early twenties, hissed like a cat. He bolted upright, dropping the mobile phone he'd been scrolling on. His canine teeth elongated and sharpened. He glanced from side to side, looking for a way to maneuver past the resolutely brandished crucifixes. Too late.

Van Helsing, Samir, and Chelsea advanced to within ten feet, taking care to avoid locking eyes with the vampire, whose gaze could mesmerize the unwary. Ted shut the ruined front door and brought up the rear. Each stride by the hunters was matched by an inhuman snarl and a retreating step by the trapped vampire, unable to abide the crosses. Once the target was backed into a corner, Quincey said, "hold."

"Whadya want?" Fury and fear played in equal measure across the vampire's face. "I haven't done shit to any of you."

Nodding at the truth of the statement, Van Helsing asked, "Who created you?"

"My parents, dumbass."

Quincy sighed. "Who turned you into a vampire, blood-breath?"

"Why do you care? There's no undo button."

"Who turned you?"

The vampire glanced past his captor's shoulder. "If you're gonna stake me anyway, I've got no reason to tell you anything."

Quincey shrugged. "This isn't a negotiation." He sheathed his stake and withdrew a small glass vial from a pocket, uncorked it with his teeth, and flicked holy water. Most of the droplets speckled the vampire's shirt, but some splattered his neck. They sizzled.

The vampire howled in agony.

The vampire hunter gave a mirthless grin. "A good vintage, based on your reaction." His mouth tightened. "Who turned you?"

The vampire seemed to be looking over Quincey's shoulder again. "Fine. You win. Edward Cullen."

Chelsea scowled. "That's a fictional vampire, asshole."

The vampire smiled and his tensed shoulders eased. "Oh, that's right. Anyway, you're outta time."

As he said that, two people burst through the front door—a petite woman with short silvery-blonde hair and a stocky Black man wearing a charcoal flat cap. Both looked to be in their early twenties. Before Ted could turn to face the intruders, the woman struck his left wrist with vampiric speed, causing the crucifix to tumble out of his grasp. The man seized Ted's neck with a single-handed grip, unbreakable by human strength. "Stand still, or I'll tear open your throat and piss down your trachea."

At Van Helsing's curt command, "hedgehog," Chelsea and Samir shifted so that the three of them stood back-to-back—Samir facing the first vampire, and Quincey and Chelsea the newcomers, crucifixes extended.

The first vampire nodded. "Ann. Dennis. I can't tell ya how glad I am you weren't late. My morning *so* didn't get off to a good start. These dudes wanted to know who turned me. What do we do about this standoff?" He tilted his head toward the humans. "Ready to negotiate now? How's this. We let your guy go, and you let me go?"

Ann frowned. "Don't be a wuss, Dave. We'll just wait them out since we can go *much* longer without sleep than humans. Then we can enjoy some tasty snacks."

"Guns," ordered Quincey, sheathing his stake and drawing his revolver. His comrades did the same.

Ann laughed. "Guns?" She shook her head. "What a bunch of losers. Don't you wannabe vampire hunters know that bullets, even silver ones, can't kill us? So sad for you."

As Ann monologued, Van Helsing made eye contact with Ted, who sighed in resignation and gave a nearly imperceptible nod. "Samir, fire!" ordered Ted.

The big man fired twice, shots booming in the enclosed space. The rounds struck the left side of Dave's chest at two-thousand feet per second.

"She told you bullets are useless. After I drain you, I'm gonna tear you to small bloodless pieces!" snarled Dennis.

"Who's using bullets?" asked Quincey, one eyebrow raised.

Dennis and Ann's bloodshot eyes widened when Dave's wounds sizzled and he howled in agony. His skin flaked, releasing a foul stench as it turned to ash and collapsed into a pile along with his clothing. Dave's soul departed for Hell.

Van Helsing hefted his revolver. "These bad boys fire half-inch-diameter magnum rounds of sharpened Brazilian olive wood. Flying stakes to unbind the dark magic that animates vampires. So sad for you. Samir and Chelsea, weapons free."

He and the others opened fire, careful not to hit Ted.

Ann dodged, but one round pierced her abdomen, sizzling. She shrieked in pain, slipping behind Dennis. There is no loyalty among the undead.

A shot from Chelsea struck Dennis's right shoulder. He roared and flexed, snapping Ted's neck, but still held him upright as a shield.

"Shit. Flank them!" barked Quincey.

"Fuck this," said Ann. "Let's fly." She transformed into a bat and flitted out the front door. Dennis did the same, the bats' irregular flight pattern saving them from a hail of flying stakes.

Ted's body tumbled limply to the carpet.

"Chelsea, check Ted," ordered Van Helsing, forcing down his rage and sorrow. "Samir, guard the door." He turned and scooped up Dave's mobile phone. "Yes! Got you, motherfuckers." Quincey set the screen lock to off and disabled the "Find My Device" feature.

"Guys, Ted's gone," whispered Chelsea between sobs.

His face red with fury, the lead vampire hunter grimaced. "We're gonna find them and end them." A tear trickled down his cheek. "Samir, help me wrap poor Ted in a rug while Chelsea checks the house for any other leads."

A quick search by Chelsea failed to discover any useful intelligence.

Samir backed the van down the driveway, shoulders stooped by the death of a comrade.

Somberly, Quincey and Samir carried their valiant comrade to the van as Chelsea opened its rear doors.

Quincey sat in the passenger seat. "Let's take a moment to honor Ted." The three bowed their heads. "Oh, Lord, we beseech you to have mercy on the soul of our fallen brother. He made the ultimate sacrifice to help rid Your world of evil. May his memory inspire us to be equally courageous. Amen."

Anger marred Van Helsing's face. "Let's go." As Samir drove, Quincey scrolled on the vampire's mobile phone. "Payback's coming, bloodsuckers."

9:40 a.m., October 9 – Seven Sisters, TX

After the team cleaned up, they met in the conference room of their underground base of operations. They moved in a fog, the tragedy of Ted's death weighing heavily.

"It was lucky you were able to access that vampire's phone before the screen locked," said Chelsea, fire in her eyes. "Did you uncover any leads?"

Quincey nodded. "Yeah. Looks like it's been three weeks since he's posted on social media. I searched through his friends list and found the other two vampires. Their full names are Ann Cardinal and Dennis Crosby. Seems like they're a couple." He raised the phone to show a photo of them kissing. "Interestingly, the lovebirds haven't posted anything in the last three weeks either."

Samir finished his second donut. "What you make of that?"

"Combine their young age with the fact that they spoke contemporary vernacular, I'd guess they were all turned around three weeks ago. A vampire was recruiting."

"Recruiting for what?" asked Samir.

Van Helsing shrugged. "Who knows? To look for us? We're not exactly popular among vampires."

Samir nodded. "One hundred percent! I say we make ourselves *more* unpopular with Ann and Dennis."

A grin appeared briefly on Quincey's face. "I found Ann and Dennis listed in Dave's contacts. So, I'll use his phone to text them malware hidden in a photo. Since they're new vampires, they may not be cautious. If they open the texts, my malware will hack their GPS and transmit periodic updates of their location. And then they'll be receiving some uninvited house guests."

Everyone smiled grimly at the prospect of vengeance.

Samir reached for the box of donuts. "This calls for a celebration."

Chelsea's eyebrows rose. "Your third?"

Pointing at his ample belly, Samir replied, "Girl, a body like this takes work."

After an all-nighter, Van Helsing briefed Samir and Chelsea at 7:30 a.m. in the conference room. "GPS showed Ann and Dennis moving around southern San Antonio throughout last night, and my police scanner picked up a report of a murder where the victim was bitten on the neck."

"Those fuckers were dining out," said Samir.

Quincey sipped his coffee and nodded. "That makes sense, particularly since we wounded them. They'd want fresh blood to heal faster."

"And to sleep in their coffins..." Chelsea leaned forward intently. "Tell me you found their coffins."

"Seems likely." He grinned. "GPS shows both of them in the same spot in Tilden since around 4 a.m." He showed them a satellite image of the house on his phone. "Gear up. We're going in fast and quiet. For Ted."

Leaving their car on a dirt side road of the forested Goldwell Street, Quincey, Chelsea, and Samir hiked northward a hundred yards through the trees to covertly approach the vampires' house from the side rather than via the driveway. They wore sneakers and camouflage fatigues, but were armed as before.

At the edge of the trees, they dashed fifty feet to a side door. Their expertise with lock picking made quick work of the deadbolt.

They slipped inside. Nearly shoulder to shoulder, they silently checked the ground floor.

Nothing. Quincey pointed at the staircase.

The second floor also proved empty, as did the attic.

They crept back to the ground floor. Upon a closer inspection, they found a door in the kitchen. Grinning, Chelsea pointed at the lock. Keyed locks on the *inside* of a house were a strong indicator of hiding something important...or dangerous.

Van Helsing picked the lock. He brandished his crucifix in his left hand and held a flashlight with his right. Chelsea and Samir eased open the door for Quincey, then followed, gripping crucifixes and stakes.

Halfway down the wooden stairs, he paused. A basement window offered a modest amount of illumination, but he swept his flashlight's beam around the space. The room held a typical assortment of household detritus—cardboard boxes, suitcases, and tools. But there were also two less typical fixtures—identical polished oak caskets. Quincey made eye contact with Chelsea and

Samir. When they nodded in acknowledgement, Van Helsing swapped his flashlight for a stake and continued down the stairs.

As Quincey and Chelsea neared the coffins, the last stair tread creaked under Samir's weight. They all winced and froze.

Both coffin lids eased open.

"Now!" cried Van Helsing, charging toward the left-hand coffin. As the lid opened fully, Quincey leaped, driving his stake with two hands into the snarling vampire Dennis's unbeating heart.

Dennis's face expressed shock before his body crumbled into a pile of noxious ash.

"Help!" screamed Chelsea.

The vampire Ann had managed to seize Chelsea's wrist, preventing her from striking a death blow.

Even with both hands, Chelsea could not budge Ann's rock-solid grip.

"Time to die," said Samir, looming behind Chelsea and adding his strength to hers to direct the stake gradually downward.

When Van Helsing splattered holy water on Ann's face, she screamed in agony.

Taking advantage of the vampire's distraction, Samir and Chelsea jammed the stake into Ann's chest.

"That's for Ted," spat Chelsea as Ann's body crumbled to ash.

"One hundred percent," agreed Samir. His nose wrinkled at the charnel stench.

Tension eased from three sets of shoulders.

Quincey withdrew a ziplock bag from his pocket. He removed two sacred wafers, placing one inside each coffin to spoil them for any other vampires. "Let's grab their mobile phones, and we're outta here."

Rather than head back to their base, they drove to a farmhouse east of Freer, a short-term rental acquired after the destruction of the first vampire, Dave.

Van Helsing led Samir and Chelsea into the kitchen, setting all three vampires' phones on the worn wooden table.

Chelsea picked up Ann's phone. "What good are the two new ones when they're locked?"

"None at all." Quincey smiled. "But after I use that malware I sent to remotely unlock them, well…"

Samir shook his head in admiration. "Remind me never to piss you off."

After five minutes of scrolling on the phones, Quincey leaned back into his chair. "Damn."

"Care to elaborate?" asked Chelsea, snacking on an energy bar.

He held up Dennis's phone, displaying a text message. It read:

Master, we have good news and bad news. The bad news is that Dave's been destroyed. The good news is that we found Van Helsing and took out one of his henchmen. We'll keep looking for their base.

"That was sent yesterday. The reply says, 'Well, done. Keep me apprised.'"

Chelsea nodded. "Master, huh? I guess we know the phone number of the guy who made the three local vampires. Anything more?"

"Oh, yeah." There was no smile on their leader's face. "All three phones have texted with their master's phone, which has a British country code. All three phones' Contacts list him as Jonathan."

Chelsea's mouth fell open. "You think it's Jonathan Harker?"

Van Helsing nodded. "Seems pretty likely. New vampires created by a British vampire sent to locate and kill us."

Samir shrugged. "Just because you destroyed his vampire wife? The guy really holds a grudge."

"Technically, it was our comrades from DNR who destroyed Mina," replied Quincey, his eyes steely. "But we lost Steve and Dan during that mission. I hold grudges, too."

"Um, shouldn't you turn off the Find My Device on the two new phones?" asked Chelsea.

He shook his head. "Nope. That would tip off Jonathan that something's wrong. Instead, I'm gonna send him an invitation he won't decline." Using Dennis's phone, he texted:

[Master, we have good news. We caught one of Van Helsing's henchmen. We're holding him at a rented farmhouse. Didn't want to keep him at our place. What should we do with him?]

While they waited for a response, the trio checked the layout of the farmhouse and planned an ambush.

Twenty minutes later, Dennis's phone chimed. Jonathan's reply read:

Bravo. Keep the prisoner healthy and unbled. I wish to interrogate him personally. What fun that shall be. Since I must cross the Atlantic by ship, I cannot be there before 19 October. You may expect me at midnight on that date. Commendable work, both of you.

"Fuck me," said Samir as the reality sunk in of an impending encounter with an older, deadlier vampire. "You think the three of us can take him?"

Quincey stared back.

"You think we can take him, right?" echoed Chelsea, standing.

"Probably, but I'm gonna get us reinforcements…DNR."

"DNR?" replied Samir. "You trust a bloodsucker and his thrall?"

Van Helsing rested a hand on Samir's shoulder. "I appreciate your concern, but DNR is like the Marines—no better friend, no worse enemy. You guys weren't on that raid, but they really saved our asses when we went after Mina Harker last year." He dialed from his own phone. It rang once.

"DNR Investigative Services. Mr. Renfield speaking. How may we help you?"

"Hello Ray. This is Quincey Van Helsing." He didn't pause for an exchange of pleasantries because they were allies only in the sense that *the enemy of my enemy is my friend.* "We've got a lead that will be *very* interesting to your boss."

"He's quite busy."

"Too busy to hear about his vampiric grandson, Jonathan Harker?" Quincey winked at Samir and Chelsea.

"Let me see if he can break away."

A minute later a smooth, deep voice said, "Hello Mr. Van Helsing. What can you tell us about Mr. Harker?"

Quincey's stomach tightened even though the speaker was far away in upstate New York. "It looks like Jonathan's hunting us and knew we were in Texas. He recently created three thralls to find us, but we, um, took care of them."

"Did you now?"

Was that a hint of approbation? wondered Quincey "We hacked their mobile phones. All three had repeatedly messaged a "Jonathan" contact, and they addressed him as "Master." I sent him a text from one of the thralls' phones, claiming to have captured one of my men."

"Clever."

"I gave him the address of a rented farmhouse east of Freer, Texas. He said he'd arrive at midnight on the nineteenth. We'll leave the thralls' phones there in case he checks their GPS. We were hoping you and Ray would help with the ambush."

"Indeed. We will help you, on one condition. Jonathan must be given a chance to change his ways. I will explain that I have mastered my predatory inclinations, only feeding from a willing assistant—never enough to kill or create a new vampire. Since his friends of old, Lucy Westenra and Arthur Holmwood, have similarly recanted, perhaps he will be persuaded."

"After you sorta lopped off Mina's head during our last encounter? Do you really think he'll sit for a cup of tea and a cozy chat?"

Dracula sighed. "No, I do not. Yet, since I seek to address my past sins, I must make the attempt. We will be there. You may text the details to Ray. Until then."

October 19 – east of Freer, TX

Quincey, Samir, and Chelsea arrived at the rented farmhouse 9:30 p.m. to prepare for the ambush of Jonathan Harker. They locked all the windows and doors except the front door. The rec room had picture windows on the west and east sides and a bookcase on its north wall, with its hallway entrance in the southwest corner. They pushed a large, overstuffed leather chair into the northwest corner. They emptied a wardrobe, lubricated its door hinges, and moved it into the southeast corner of the room. A closet on the hallway leading to the rec room was similarly emptied.

They reviewed their plan one last time.

Moths that had fluttered outside the eastern window since sundown suddenly dispersed.

At 11:30 p.m., the three vampire hunters took up their positions. Samir sat in the comfy chair, a crucifix and a revolver hidden under the seat cushion. Chelsea wrapped rope around his wrists and ankles, but didn't knot the loops, portraying him as a "hostage" of Ann and Dennis. She slipped into the wardrobe, while Quincey hid in the hallway closet.

At midnight, front door hinge squeaks and footsteps on the hardwood floor told of a punctual visitor.

Despite being prepared, Samir stiffened as a slightly built man with brown hair and brown eyes strode into the living room. Samir's eyes were drawn to the two kukri knives sheathed at the vampire's belt. Most likely, one of these had murdered Samir's vampire hunting comrades, Steve and Dan. Samir's face reddened.

The vampire paused in the center of the room, his eyes sparkling with grim humor. "Well, well. What have we here? A midnight snack, perchance? But where are my manners? Allow me to introduce myself. I am Jonathan Harker. And you are?" He paused, staring, but Samir averted his eyes to avoid falling under the vampire's spell.

"No name? No matter." The vampire waved his hand dismissively. "Your name is less important than that of Van Helsing's. Tell me where he is, and I will spare your life."

Samir didn't respond to the lie.

Jonathan smiled. "I shall enjoy watching my thralls get the answer out of you. Where are they, by the way? Upstairs?" He raised his voice. "Mr. Crosby? Ms. Cardinal?"

"I'm afraid Dennis isn't available," said Quincey, standing at the room entrance with a crucifix in his left hand and a pistol in his right.

"And neither is Ann," added Chelsea emerging from the wardrobe, also with a crucifix and revolver.

"Broke into the wrong goddamn rec room, didn't ya?" said Samir, the two strands of rope now loose at his feet. He stood, armed with cross and gun like his comrades.

Harker crouched and hissed like a cornered cat. Then he straightened and laughed, his mirth so out of context as to be disconcerting. "Has no one cautioned you against meddling in the affairs of vampires? Surely, you are not so naive as to believe you have caught me unawares?"

The two windows shattered inward. Quick as a snake, Van Helsing dived and rolled toward Samir, barely dodging the vampire who had smashed shoulder-first through the western window.

Chelsea was slower to react. The vampire crashing through the eastern window snapped a kick to her left wrist, sending her cross tumbling across the room. A blurred slash of his right hand across her slender neck severed her left carotid artery and trachea. She gasped and fell to the flow, spasming in agony as her life blood pumped onto the hardwood floor.

"No!" screamed Quincey. "Not Chelsea." He yanked the detonator from his jacket pocket and triggered the claymore directional anti-personnel mine they had installed in the bookcase at the center of the north wall. "Burn in hell!"

WHOOMP!

The vampire hunters had previously replaced the mine's seven hundred eighth-inch-diameter steel balls with two hundred black ironwood flechettes—any of which would destroy a vampire if it pierced its unbeating heart.

The three vampires screamed in agony. Wounds on arms, legs, and face steamed. But no flechettes protruded from the vampires' torsos.

As Samir readied himself to sprint to Chelsea, Quincey put a restraining hand on his shoulder. "Don't. They're wearing body armor."

Jonathan was the first to regain his composure, offering a disdainful smirk and calmly plucking a flechette from his right cheek. The wound healed within seconds. "As I said…"

"I'm gonna shred these fuckers!" screamed one of the vampires, writhing in pain from flechettes in his left arm and leg.

"You will await my command, Martin," admonished Jonathan. "They are trapped, and I wish to interrogate them… before we feed."

Quincey and Samir brandished their crucifixes, their backs to the northwest corner so they couldn't be outflanked. It was a standoff…until eventual exhaustion would force them to drop their guard.

Jonathan turned his leonine gaze on Van Helsing and scowled. "I recognize you from the attack on my mansion."

He put on a brave face, determined not to give his enemy the satisfaction of seeing his fear. "Quincey Van Helsing, the latest in a long line of vampire hunters."

Jonathan chuckled. "Latest…and soon to be last. Tell me the names of your henchmen who are not present tonight."

"Why would I do that, you soulless leech?"

"Name-calling? Really? Are we not adults? If you give me the information I seek, it will mean a swift and relatively painless death for you and your oversized comrade. If not…" He let the obvious alternative hang in the air unspoken. "So, what will—"

Rumbling wolf growls interrupted Jonathan's question.

When the three vampires turned to face the newcomers, Quincey and Samir holstered their pistols and withdrew silver flasks from their pockets.

Three large gray wolves stood next to a man with short black hair and deep eyes that suggested an age belied by his trim physique. He wore a black sweatsuit, black sneakers, and incongruously carried an ivory-handled wooden cane. "Mr. Harker," said Dracula. "I offer you a choice between changing your ways… or perishing. Will you—"

"I WILL NOT!" snarled Jonathan. "You murdered my wife! Martin, kill the humans. Brandon, help me destroy Dracula."

Martin drew a 9mm Glock 17 from his belt and opened fire at the vampire hunters, who dived for cover. He got off three rounds. One bullet missed, one struck the ceramic armor plate under Quincey's shirt, and the third punched through Samir's left bicep.

Van Helsing flicked holy water on Martin. The drops of holy water acted like acid, causing intense burning pain. It wouldn't destroy him, but he couldn't recover quickly like he could from gunshots.

Brandon unsheathed two wooden stakes and charged at Dracula.

The three wolves growled and leaped at Jonathan before he could advance. They snapped their jaws, trying to clamp down on limbs moving at inhuman speed.

With the dual advantages of his longer cane and decades of kendo training, Dracula landed a blow on Brandon's right wrist, causing him to drop one stake. Without pausing, Dracula pivoted and drove the cane's narrow end into Brandon's right eye socket. While not a lethal blow to a vampire, the painful distraction afforded Dracula the split second he needed to seize the vampire in a front headlock. With a mighty jerk, Dracula snapped Brandon's neck. Again, the injury was not lethal to a vampire, but resulted in temporary paralysis. Dracula didn't waste those few seconds. He tore off the chest plate of Brandon's armor, snatched a fallen wooden stake, and plunged it into the vampire's heart.

Brandon's death scream drew Martin's attention away from Quincey and Samir. When Brandon's body collapsed into noisome ash, Martin muttered, "Fuck this." He turned himself into a dense mist and drifted out the smashed eastern window. Visible in the moonlight, he floated away from the house.

Ray Renfield, Dracula's assistant and former U.S. Army Ranger, crouched behind a hedge, awaiting this possibility. He stood and let loose with a Throwflame ARC commercial flamethrower. A gout of fire engulfed the vampire's mist form. A tormented ghostly howl marked Martin's passage into hell. Ray set down the flamethrower, drew his revolver, and took up an overwatch position outside the eastern window.

By that time, Jonathan had killed the three wolves, although the fight left him with limbs torn by claws and teeth. These healed as he stared with rabid fury at Dracula. Wolf blood dripped from the blades of his two kukris quivering with Jonathan's barely contained rage.

Dracula cooly drew a slender sword hidden in his cane as Jonathan roared and charged.

The vampires battled, their movements so fast they blurred in Quincey's vision. Slashing kukris clanged against sword blade or lopped off sections of the cane Dracula wielded in his left hand. Dracula's face remained calm, while Jonathan's was a rictus of rage.

An impossibly fast kukri slashed Dracula's left forearm, causing him to drop the cane. Sensing that victory and vengeance were at hand, Jonathan paused, took a step back, and smiled. "Finally. Time to die and grant me my revenge, Dracula."

BAM! BAM!

Jonathan staggered back a half step, his ceramic chest armor foiling the hardwood bullets fired by Renfield from the window. He sneered. "Be patient, Mr. Renfield. I shall turn my attention to you in due—"

BAM!

A hardwood bullet fired by Van Helsing slammed into the back of Jonathan's head. "For Chelsea!" Not fatal to a vampire, but the painful distraction afforded a narrow window of opportunity.

Dracula seized his chance. Almost too fast to see, he leaped forward and slashed horizontally.

Jonathan's severed head tumbled to the floor as his body collapsed. Both pieces crumbled into ash.

Quincey holstered his pistol gave a grim nod of thanks to Dracula. "Strange bedfellows, but we get the job done." He cut a strip of cloth from his jacket and pivoted to give aid to his wounded comrade.

Samir grunted as Van Helsing tied the tourniquet on his arm. "Poor Chelsea."

Nodding, Quincey said, "She will be greatly missed. Let's take a moment." He and Samir bowed their heads. "Oh, Lord, we beseech you to have mercy on the soul of our fallen sister. She made the ultimate sacrifice to help rid Your world of evil. May her memory inspire us to be equally courageous. Amen."

"I'm gonna get a blanket so we can bring Chelsea home," said Samir. "May Harker burn in hell for taking her from us."

Renfield leaned in the eastern window. "Roger that. Never bring kukris to a sword fight."

Author's Note

This is the latest story of occult detectives, Dracula and Ray Renfield, whose covert exploits are documented in "Norsemen Cruise Line," *Dracula Beyond Stoker (DBS) issue #1*, "Don't Mess With a Renfield," *DBS #2*, "Loose End," *DBS #3*, "Cold Shoulders," *DBS #4*, "Smitten," *DBS #5*, and "Alliance of Convenience," *DBS #7*.

Henry Herz has written for *Daily Science Fiction, Weird Tales, Pseudopod, Metastellar, Titan Books, Highlights for Children, Ladybug Magazine,* and anthologies from Penguin-Random House, Albert Whitman, Blackstone Publishing, Third Flatiron, Brigids Gate Press, Air and Nothingness Press, Baen Books, *Dracula Beyond Stoker,* and elsewhere. He's edited ten anthologies and written fourteen picture books. www.henryherz.com

Van Helsing Syndrome
By Connor Boyle

Incident Summary Report: 2024-003701
Reporting Officer: David Romero

At 22:20 on May 25, 2024, while performing a foot patrol in the Pueblo Memorial section of Cortez Park, I visually identified an unknown white male concealing himself in an area of low bushes. Having foreknowledge of the area as a frequent site for the sale of illegal narcotics, as well as the location of a recent string of violent murders, I approached the subject with the intention of performing a cursory interview and ascertaining the state of his sobriety. Upon noticing my approach, the subject proceeded to flee on foot. Following a brief pursuit, I was able to subdue the subject and place him in handcuffs. I then called for backup support and proceeded to search the subject's black Jansport backpack for weapons or other contraband. From the backpack, I recovered four sharpened pieces of wood and one rubber headed mallet.

Detective Sergeant Caroline Lewis arrived on scene at 22:42 to assume custody of the arrestee, identified as Henry Rostock from a New Mexico state driver's license.

Audio log transcribed from body camera of Officer David Romero

22:25.13 : Well, you got me. What took you so long?

22:25.16: What do you mean? Tell me who it is I got, sir.

22:25.21: [laughter] The Duke City Staker. I'm the guy you've been looking for.

"Garlic, holy water, crucifixes, they're all effective deterrents, but only sunlight or a stake in the heart can kill a vampire."

Henry Rostock sat with his legs crossed in front of him, a limp wrist hung over a bent knee. *Like he's being interviewed by Dick Cavett,* thought Detective Lewis.

It was hard to believe he had murdered four people.

"How did you pick them?"

Up until tonight, Lewis had never seen Special Agent Kessler in person. He'd existed only as a voice on the phone during her weekly teleconference with the feds. Now that he was here, Lewis found herself oddly entranced by his baritone voice. It was far more soothing in person.

"I picked them because they were vampires," said Rostock.

"What Agent Kessler means to ask," said Lewis, "is what made you think they were vampires?"

"When they try to rip your throat out, it's a pretty good tell," said Rostock. "Which is to say that I let them come to me. I make myself vulnerable, they attack, and I respond."

A vigilante mindset, thought Lewis. *He picks fights. Incites, so he can respond with deadly force.*

Rostock continued. "Vampires go for the low hanging fruit. The people who you might refer to as the less dead. Vagrants, prostitutes, addicts. A vampire kills a rich attorney in Nob Hill, someone's going to ask questions. But if they drain a few junkies in a city park, nobody bats an eye. To say nothing of the fact that a junkie isn't going to put up much of a fight."

"So you hunt where the vampires hunt," said Lewis. "You disguise yourself as the weak antelope at the watering hole, hope a vampire pegs you as easy prey, then you go on the attack."

Rostock nodded.

The term for such predatory behavior in nature, Lewis remembered from her college biology class, was *aggressive mimicry*. Her professor had pointed to the anglerfish as a prime example. Evolution had equipped the anglerfish with a bioluminescent appendage that, to other marine life, looked like a tasty worm. When a smaller predator came in to devour the worm, they, in turn, were devoured by the anglerfish.

She wondered if there would be any value in pointing out the similarities between Rostock's behavior and that of the anglerfish.

Probably not.

"Mr. Dow was the exception," said Rostock. "We both happened to be drinking at the Silversmith Lodge. I saw him and I just knew. You spend enough time around vampires and you can spot them easily. It's like a sixth sense. I told him we should take a walk, that it was a nice night. I think he thought I was trying to pick him up. But in reality, it was him who was trying to pick me up, but not for sex. Rather, he wanted me for a midnight snack."

"Did he attack you?" asked Lewis.

"No, it didn't get that far."

"But if he never attacked you, how could you be sure he was a vampire?"

"There are ways to tell," said Rostock. "An inability to cast a reflection or a shadow or be photographed. I snapped a photo with my cellphone when he wasn't looking, just to make sure I was right."

"The medical examiner took plenty of photos of the victims' bodies," said Kessler. "Of Dow's and the others. I've seen them. Those cadavers photograph just fine."

"When a vampire is disposed of it reverts back to its pre-vampiric state just before death. Final death, that is. All traces of vampirism disappear when they die for the last time, including the inability to be photographed."

"Did anyone help you?" asked Kessler. "Robin Dow was a strong guy. Hard to believe you could handle him by yourself."

"No," said Rostock flatly. "Hunters work alone."

" I want to show you something," said Lewis, reaching into her jacket pocket and removing her cell phone. She tapped the touch screen several times, then slid the phone in front of Rostock.

"This is video of Alec Somoski leaving his gym close to midnight."

Rostock hunched over the screen and watched. His eyes blank and emotionless as the video ran its length, showing the 6'2" Somoski jogging lightly through the parking lot of Elite MMA Academy. The video came to an end just as Somoski stepped out of range of the camera.

"You remember Alec, right?"

Rostock leaned back in his chair, nodded.

"How do you explain the video then?"

"If that video is real," said Rostock, "and I'm not convinced that it is, but supposing it's real, then I've made a horrible mistake."

"That's putting it lightly," said Kessler.

"However," continued Rostock, "if it is real, it also means that Mr. Somoski is a martyr in a battle that has been ongoing since the dawn of man, and that he is now with the angels and saints in Heaven."

At midnight, the investigators excused themselves and retired to Lewis' office. Lewis sat in her rolling chair and rested her feet on the edge of her desk. Kessler performed an overhead stretch and let out a deep yawn.

"Hell of a story," said Lewis.

"He's a rare bird," said Kessler, "but not singular. Our forensic psych people call it Van Helsing Syndrome."

"Van Helsing like the guy from *Dracula*," said Lewis. "Clever."

"It's a combination of the vision killer and mission killer subgroups, although there's also a clear psychosexual dynamic. The use of a stake, for example. It's not just a prop in the offender's hero fantasy, but also an important phallic prosthetic. We believe the desire to role play as a vampire hunter stems from feelings of sexual impotence."

Lewis sipped her coffee. It was her third of the night. She'd have to slow it down if she wanted to sleep sometime in the next century.

"We've seen half a dozen cases nationwide in the past two years," continued Kessler. "All more or less the same MO. All used stakes. All said the people they killed were vampires."

"Jesus Christ," said Lewis. "You think there's a connection?"

"That's what we've been trying to figure out," said Kessler. "So far we haven't been able to identify any personal connection between offenders."

"Maybe they were all radicalized by the same source. An Internet forum or something like that."

"Maybe," said Kessler.

"Regardless, if he's authentically delusional, that raises another issue," said Lewis.

Kessler stared at his wingtip shoes for a moment.

"Non compos mentos. It did occur to me."

"We could have a shrink talk to him. Probably want to do that before he lawyers up."

"You know any sympathetic shrinks awake at midnight?" asked Kessler.

"Not any sober ones," said Lewis.

"There's a field office in Durango. I think I can get the Denver psych unit to meet me there tonight."

"What about his arraignment?"

"We can hold him for seventy-two hours before he needs to go before a judge. I'll have him back before then."

Lewis made to protest, but stopped. If the feds wanted to interview Rostock using their own shrinks, that's what they were going to do. No use in getting into a pissing match over it. Besides, Lewis didn't like the idea of the guy getting off on an insanity plea, not that he'd live an enviable existence spending the rest of his days in a state funded psychiatric hospital. And if the Bureau's shrinks could dismantle the groundwork of such a plea, then a temporary exchange of custody was an inconvenience she'd have to put up with.

"I'll get started on the paperwork," said Lewis.

Thirty minutes later, she watched as Kessler's Lincoln Town Car pulled out of the parking lot of Albuquerque PD's downtown station.

Rostock turned in the backseat and gave her a slight smile. *Like the cat that ate the canary,* thought Lewis.

The man was, in Lewis' estimation, authentically delusional. Henry Rostock's world was occupied by bloodthirsty vampires, and it was his duty to kill them. He was as batshit crazy as they came, but he was not a liar. At least not entirely. There was one thing he'd said that she couldn't quite let go of. It remained with her like a piece of meat stuck in her teeth.

Hunters work alone.

That one had made her internal polygraph machine jump.

Rostock peered in the rearview mirror and saw his own grimy, tired visage staring back. He needed a hot shower and a toothbrush. With his hands and legs secured, he could barely move more than a few inches in either direction. It would be a long ride, made even longer by the muscle cramps that were beginning to set in.

His eyes floated from his own face to the reflection of the driver's seat.

"I've always thought someone like you must exist."

"Someone like me?" repeated Kessler, glancing up at the rearview.

Where Kessler's upper body should have been reflected, Rostock saw nothing but an empty leather seat. An invisible man was serving as his chauffeur tonight.

"Someone who hunts the hunters," said Rostock. "The Van Helsing of the other side."

Kessler shrugged.

Both men were silent for the next two hours as they passed through Bernalillo and Santa Fe, then followed I-25 into the winding foothills of the Sangre de Cristos Mountains. Once the lights of Wagon Mound had faded behind them, a blanketing darkness crept down from the surrounding mountains, consuming everything but the short patch of concrete illuminated in the Town Car's headlights. Kessler felt as if he was driving along the bottom of the ocean rather than the high desert.

"Where are you taking me?" asked Rostock.

"We're going to a field office in Durango. We've got a team of people meeting us there. They want to ask you some questions."

"You mean torturers," said Rostock.

Kessler grinned. "Call them what you like. Some of them are psychiatrists. Maybe they can help."

They passed a buckshot-riddled sign reading: RATON PASS, NO EXIT FOR 2 MILES.

In the distance, before the highway dipped into another valley between two overhanging mesas, a pin prick of light moved along the road. Like a ripe glowworm floating in the darkness.

"I'm curious about your hunting methods," said Kessler. "There were a few things we touched upon in our interview that I'd like to discuss more, if you're okay with that."

"You want to know about the network," said Rostock. "About the other active hunters."

Kessler glanced over his shoulder, then back to the road.

"Is there a network?"

"We don't use that word," said Rostock. "Have you ever heard the name Ludwig Von Kruger?"

Kessler's head turned slightly again. "It sounds vaguely familiar."

"He was Van Helsing's tutor," said Rostock.

"I didn't know Van Helsing had a tutor."

"He did," said Rostock. "They met at the University of Amsterdam. It was Dr. Von Kruger who instructed Van Helsing in the methods of vampire hunting. And it was Von Kruger who served as Van Helsing's handler during the hunt for Count Dracula. Stoker's decision to forego any mention of Dr. Von Kruger in his novel was, I believe, a strategic omission."

The light Kessler had seen before now blossomed into a glowing orb. Kessler squinted. It wasn't one light he was seeing, but many. Multiple fist-sized lanterns strung like a garland across the width of the road.

"We are a fraternity," continued Rostock. "And for each of us younger hunters, there's always a handler. An older hunter who provides counsel on strategy and technique. Also someone to help when we're in a bind."

Kessler could see it clearly now in the headlights. Parked crosswise across both lanes was an older model pickup. Arranged in front of it was a series of jersey barricades threaded with heavy duty shop lights.

Lewis brought the Town Car to a slow stop less than ten feet from the barricade.

A tall, stooped man with long, stringy hair emerged from the darkness beside the truck, positioning himself in Kessler's headlights. Kessler could make out a shotgun slung in the crook of the man's pencil-thin arm.

"We've got a team of people who'd like to speak to you, too," said Rostock. "We're curious about your network, as it were. Those who hunt the hunters."

The stooped man held out one clenched fist holding what looked to Kessler like a television remote. A quick motion of his thumb brought to life a glowing crucifix, strewn with red and white Christmas bulbs, in the bed of the pickup.

Kessler brought a hand before his face. The brightness of the crucifix stung at the backs of his eyes.

The man with the shotgun approached the driver's side window, leveling the barrel of the weapon at Kessler's head.

"Open the door, slowly," the muffled voice said, "or I'll blow your head off."

"Better do what he says," said Rostock.

"I'm not a vampire," said Kessler. "Just think about what you're doing for a minute."

"I wonder how long it takes for a vampire's head to grow back," said Rostock. "Perhaps we'll find out tonight."

Kessler's nails clattered against the plastic siding of the passenger door as he fumbled for the lock.

The door opened and a fist grasped Kessler round the collar, pulling him out onto the cold and damp road.

Kessler seethed with anger and fear. His incisors found the tip of his tongue and bit down hard. The coppery taste of blood sobered him briefly.

"You're making a mistake," he managed through clenched teeth. "You're both crazy."

"Open your eyes," the tall man ordered, pressing the barrel of the shotgun against Kessler's scalp.

Kessler willed his eyes to open, but couldn't. Just a slight glimpse of the glaring cruciform sent an acid pain burning through his skull.

Kessler pulled more blood into his throat, commanding himself to stand up. To do something. Do anything. Go for the man's gun.

Go for his throat.

Connor Boyle saw *Creature from the Black Lagoon* at a very young age and has been obsessed with monsters ever since. His work has appeared in the aquatic horror anthology *Rampage on the Reef*, the mall horror anthology *Escalators to Hell*, the yardsale horror anthology *Curbside Curses*, and in *Starlite Pulp Review #5*. He is also the editor and publisher of *The Orbit Drive-In Zine*. He lives in Santa Fe, New Mexico.

Poison in the Darkness
By Rita Oakes

I

1846

The room was small, the furnishings spare: a dressing table with mirror, a straight-backed chair, a narrow, rumpled bed devoid of bedcurtains, a faded rug that might have been pretty once. The single window was shuttered, closed against the damp night air. The oil lamps, shaded with beaded glass, gave off a pink-gold light that should have lent an air of mystery to the chamber, but instead only depressed him. The young Abraham Van Helsing studied the light to avoid looking at the woman.

"You're shy," she said. "That's all right. I like shy young men."

She was paid to like men, shy or not.

"And handsome," she said. "The young sir is very handsome."

This was not true. He was too gangly, for one thing. Recently his knees and elbows had developed a life of their own, leaving him graceless and a hazard to his mother's Dresden porcelain. A ridiculous fuzz had begun to sprout upon his cheeks. His skin, flawless a mere six months ago, had erupted with acne. No, he was anything but handsome. And he dearly wished he could be elsewhere. Standing a round of beer for his friends, perhaps. Or back home with his nose in a book.

"My—my father sent me," he said, wincing at the stammer and the naked fear in his voice.

She nodded, brushed his cheek with one finger. "Many are nervous the first time," she said, "but I can tell that you and I are going to be great friends."

She was clad in corset and petticoat. The corset pushed her breasts high. The tops peeked in grapefruit-sized mounds above a sheer bodice.

She took his hand, studied the ragged fingernails a moment, the narrow sliver of dried blood upon his thumb where, under the falsely genial gaze of his father in the coach, he had worried at a cuticle. "A gentleman of quality should take better care of his hands," she said.

"I know." His face grew warm. "I can't help it."

"Never mind." She placed his hand upon her breast. Soft. Smooth. Like perfectly kneaded bread dough. Warm, too. Pleasant. Perhaps he would get through this without embarrassing himself too badly. Then he could go home. Back to his studies.

She pulled away, and he let his hand fall to his side. She drew the chair back from her dressing table, placed a foot upon it, jutting out bosom and one hip. "Will you help me with my stockings?"

She lifted her petticoat slowly, past ankle and knee. Van Helsing swallowed, forced himself forward.

Her stockings were wrinkled, spotted a little with mud. Under her guidance, he reached his hand under the petticoat, began to roll down the coarsely knit stocking. She shifted position, and he removed that one as well. She had dimpled knees. The lamplight showed a sprinkling of dark hair upon her calves. Van Helsing caught an odor from under her clothing, something heavier and less sweet than the cloying perfume she wore, something of sweat and brine and musk and mystery. He wasn't sure he liked it. Yet he felt a stirring within his breeches, a quickening of his breath. She smiled at him.

"Thank you," she said. She unfastened his coat, helped him shrug out of it. She passed her hand over his groin lightly, teasingly, before she unbuttoned and dropped the front of his breeches, fishing the blind snake within free with practiced fingers. She spat upon her palm and coaxed his member to reluctant life.

She drew him to the bed and hoisted her petticoats.

He stared. He'd never seen a woman's privates before. There was hair between her thighs. The Greek and Roman statues he'd seen in museums did not have hair. Not there. Perhaps this woman was aberrant. His erection wilted.

She sighed softly, reached for him again. "Come, my young sir, I'll not bite."

He closed his eyes.

She stroked him back to stiffness, guided him inside the coarse thatch between her legs. She pressed his face to her breast.

He spent himself quickly. She released him. He dressed as swiftly as trembling hands would permit. He wanted to be rid of her, be rid of the sour, vaguely animal odor that rose from her skin, be rid of the stickiness that had come from her, or from himself, or from their commingling, be rid of the lingering sense of suffocation and shame. This was what it meant to be a man? If so, he found little to recommend it. Upon her dressing table he left the coin his father had given him.

II

1855

Van Helsing entered the vast study, which looked out on the botanical gardens of the University of Leyden. Lined on three sides with bookshelves from floor to ceiling, the room housed ancient herbals, early studies of anatomy, treatises on fungi, pharmacology, beekeeping. Van Helsing had a particular love for this room, its vaguely musty odor of old parchment, oiled leather, centuries of accumulated knowledge. He'd always been bookish, and there were tomes enough here, ancient and modern, to keep him in contented study for centuries.

But it was not the room alone he loved.

Miss Marieke Boerhaave sat at a long, dark table near the window, where dust motes danced in a slant of late afternoon light. He admired the graceful curve of her neck as she bent, a little near-sightedly, over her task, delicately pinning a butterfly to a mounting board.

Like her distinguished ancestor, Hermann Boerhaave, Marieke possessed a keen mind. Unlike him, she devoted her studies not to medicine or botany, but to entomology. Lepidoptera. Butterflies.

People said Marieke had the mind of a man. Van Helsing imagined her as a gravely solemn child, curious but always apart, as he had so often felt apart.

As a young woman, she remained grave, but not humorless. Van Helsing had managed to coax a smile from her more than once, and that smile warmed better than the aged and potent jenever he sometimes sipped when the evenings grew damp and chill.

Something inside his stomach fluttered, as if her butterflies had magically materialized inside him. Or perhaps the eels he had dined on earlier disagreed with him.

He studied her a moment longer in silence, his throat tight. He had no wish to disturb her until she finished her task. The stark white of her pinafore contrasted pleasantly with her gown of sober gray silk. She took up a pen, dipped it into the inkwell, wrote a label for the specimen in a neat hand.

"The purple emperor," he said. More blue than purple, the butterfly possessed a startling iridescence when illumined by a shaft of sunlight from the window. Splotches of white like careless drips of paint countered dusky brown at the edges of the wings. "Beautiful," he said.

She glanced at him, nodded. "Apatura iris. A fine specimen of Nymphalidae."

"Some say the butterfly carries messages from Heaven. Others that it represents the soul in flight after death."

"You are the repository of a great deal of fanciful information, Doctor Van Helsing," she said.

So much was true. He was indiscriminate in his tastes, devouring myth as much as mathematics, literature as much as law, religion as much as science. He filed all away in his voracious mind, great truths and trivia, until such time as he might need them. "Is that a condemnation?" he asked. The fluttering in his stomach grew worse. He could not bear it if she should think him a fool.

She considered a long moment before she answered. "No."

"Will you take a turn with me through the gardens?"

He expected her to refuse. And then his carefully rehearsed speech would go unsaid, his hopes no more to fly than the dead butterfly mounted upon the table before her.

"Yes," she said. "I should enjoy a walk."

Spring in the Low Countries, and tulips—red, yellow, pink, white splashed with red, red flamed with yellow—nodded their heads in a breeze scented with distant rain. Hyacinth and narcissus held somewhat lesser stature. The grass, deeply green, looked as if it had been trimmed with scissors, and met the stone path neatly.

They walked side by side in silence. The wind brought a pleasing flush to Marieke's cheek, toyed with the gray silk ribbon of her bonnet. She paused a moment, observing a small orange, black, and cream-colored butterfly at rest upon a hyacinth. "Aglais uriticae," she said. The tortoise-shell butterfly flitted away. Van Helsing thought it more pleasant to watch the insects in flight than to see them killed, dried, and pinned, but would not risk her scorn by saying so.

"I have been offered a position in Amsterdam," he said. "I will be able to continue my research there."

"Congratulations."

"The salary will not make me rich, but with sufficient frugality, will permit the maintenance of a comfortable household."

"Then you are indeed fortunate."

Fortunate? Yes. Or rather, he might be. He studied the spiked petals of the brilliant red and yellow Duc van Tol tulip. A very ancient hybrid. Nearby nodded a patch of Rembrandts in white and red. Like blood splashed on snow, he thought. What if she should refuse him? What then? The news of his leaving certainly seemed to cause her no distress. But then, it wouldn't. She was not the sort to succumb to a fit of vapors. He would not find himself so drawn to her if she were.

"Miss Boerhaave—?"

"Yes?"

"I should esteem it a very great honor if you were to consent to become my wife."

She fixed him with a look as sharp as the pins she used to transfix her specimens. He held his breath. His fingers twitched a little, the old longing to gnaw upon his fingernails very strong, though he had broken himself of the habit long ago. After all, who would trust a physician with ragged nails and torn cuticles?

"Very well," she said.

III
1869

I did love him once. Alone of all men, he did not treat me as a brainless ninny whose only concern should be a new frock or a filled dance card. He did not look at me as if I'd sprouted two heads when I spoke of matters scientific. He was a good man, a kindly man, though given sometimes to flights of fanciful thinking, despite the rigors of both medicine and law. Brilliant, in his way, but as fascinated by superstition as by science. Sometimes his logic abandoned him altogether.

When he asked me to marry him, I said yes. My suitors had been few enough, and I neared that age when I began to fear I should be a spinster forever.

It was not so much I desired a home and family of my own, but I had grown weary of the pitying glances and shaking heads of my relatives, which constrained me as fully as the stays of my corset.

He did not mind my somewhat cool nature, my readings of Linnaeus or Darwin, my long hours observing the minute world of insects. My specialty was Lepidoptera, and I suppose that a genteel enough hobby, even for the fair sex.

We were happy. For a time. I came to the marriage bed with more curiosity than fear. He was awkward, unpracticed I think, and touchingly apologetic for making me submit to embraces he thought I must find distasteful.

I did not find them so, though I will confess disappointment that so momentous an experience proved dull and somewhat silly. Surely, I thought, there was more to the union of flesh and soul than this? What of the breathless passion of the poets?

Poets lie, I decided. No matter. I still had Lepidoptera.

Had I been a man, I should have traveled to Sumatra or Madagascar to collect the largest, most colorful specimens of Saturniidae. As it was, I contented myself with journals and correspondence. I collected the exotics captured by others' nets.

The years passed. I conceived a son and brought him to term without undue difficulty. Jeröen was a joy to us both, sunny-natured and affectionate. Tender of heart, perhaps excessively so, for he always wept when I put my butterflies into the killing jar, or when I later pinned them through the thorax upon the mounting board for display.

I had many specimens—large, iridescent reds and greens shipped to me from the tropics, as well as the smaller species more commonly seen in our Dutch gardens. Framed, they made a beautiful display lining the stairwell, and in the room where I studied. Van had one upon the desk in his downstairs study, the common apatura iris, the purple emperor, which I had been mounting the day he proposed to me.

We were happy, as I said. Van proved a generous husband, liberal to me with gifts of flowers, books, and chocolates. He was an attentive, loving father and missed Jeröen terribly when the boy went away to school. Truthfully, he missed the boy more than I, for Jeröen had a horror of the things I found most fascinating. Never think I did not love my son, for I did. But I rarely knew what to say to him.

One Thursday afternoon, returning from errands, a sudden rain shower forced me into a bookshop. The sun had long set before the rain slowed to the merest drizzle and I turned my steps homeward.

She stood beneath the gaslight, pale, utterly drenched, quite wretched looking. Her clothes were of good quality, or I would not have paused. I asked if she were ill. She looked faint, and I took her hand. Quite chill, it was.

"Come," I said, "my husband is a physician. You shall have a glass of sherry and a warm fire, and he shall put you to rights."

"You are very kind," she said. Her Dutch had a charming accent. Italian, I thought. My heart swelled with pity for one so far from home and alone.

The servants were away. I always gave them Thursday evenings free. I quite liked the quiet of an empty house. Jeröen was at school until the next holiday. Van had not yet returned from his rounds at the hospital.

"You must get out of those wet things," I said, and brought her towels and a dressing gown. I poured sherry for her, but she left the glass untouched.

She was beautiful, full of form, pale as marble. Aphrodite, I fancied, and dismissed the notion as something Van would have thought. But in truth, my husband was far from my mind. I felt a sudden weakness in the knees and a rush of pleasure such as sometimes had happened when Jeröen was an infant and suckled at my breast.

She took the dressing gown but draped it over a chair. She toweled her hair dry. Blonde, though dark with dampness. Dark honey shining with points of firelight. My throat felt tight.
"Will you not dress?" I said, "my husband—"

"Does not please you."

Stung, I said, "Of course, he pleases me. He is a brilliant man. He—"

Lips brushed mine, light as a butterfly wing. I stepped back, startled, though not as appalled as I might have been.

"He lacks passion," she said, and kissed me again, more firmly. My heart drummed beneath the prison of my corset. So loud, I thought surely she must hear. My head felt light, as if I'd taken too much wine. I broke away from her, my face hot with shame.

No. Not shame. Desire.

I thought myself long immune to passion. I had science, after all. Study. My insects, coldly gassed, pinned, displayed. I had never been prone to frivolity, hysteria. I liked things measured, labeled, analyzed. I—

I wanted her. I abandoned sweet reason for this utterly new sensation of melting delight. I trembled, for my flesh could not contain this wanting. I sank to the floor, hid my face. I did not know what to do or say.

She held me, pressed my face to her bosom, stroked the nape of my neck with fingers still chilled from the storm. I had heat for us both. I kissed her, shyly, and then more boldly when she did not pull away. She loosed my hair from its severe chignon, unlaced my gown, my corset.

I felt an ache in my lower back. It had annoyed me all day, presaging the onset of my menses. My insides seemed to dissolve, and I felt the curse of Eve between my thighs. Too early. I thought I would die of shame.

I pushed her away. "I am unclean," I said.

Her nostrils flared, and she smiled. "Not to me. There is no shame in blood." She kissed me again and caressed me with great tenderness. The ache vanished. Pleasure only remained.

She left before Van returned home, pledging to return to me on Thursday next. I drew on the dressing gown, drank the untouched sherry.

Van was worried at my preoccupation that evening, my disordered hair, my flushed skin. Doctor that he was, he bled me, far more painfully than she had done, and put me to bed. It was only when he climbed carefully into the bed beside me that the thought came to me I was an adulteress. I began to weep, I who never wept, and alarmed him further. He held me, and stroked my hair, and asked if I had pain. He had laudanum below, in his apothecary cabinet, but I shook my head and clung to him, clung to this good man, whom I had betrayed.

I abandoned Lepidoptera. Caterina was far more exotic. I felt shattered by my passions, and yet curiously freed by them. Caterina visited me weekly when servants and husband were away. How precious our time together, how tender.

She was more than a woman—I had forgotten to mention that, I think. Centuries older than I, but forever young, and unfettered by convention. There is, I am sure, a scientific explanation for creatures such as she, but Caterina refused to submit to microscopic analysis. "I am not one of your specimens," she would say and then kiss me.

Yes, she drank blood. She killed sometimes. That is the nature of a predator. But to me, she remained unfailingly tender, taught me to take as much pleasure in the flesh as I had always taken in the mind. I realized I had been only half alive before she came to me.

My only regret was my continued deception of that good man, my husband. It was almost a relief to me when he returned home earlier than expected and discovered us in flagrante delicto.

Such a cry of grief he made, I feared for his reason.

Caterina sprang upon him. He struggled but could not free himself of her unnatural strength. Her eyes had gone that strange red that told of hunger or rage. She could break him like a dry stick.

"You must not hurt him," I said, drawing on a dressing gown in haste. I, his wife, had hurt him deeply enough.

"Why ever not?" As I said, she could be cruel.

"Because I ask it."

She called me a fool. She drank from him, deeply until he swooned, but for my sake, she let him live. And a little bloodletting is good for you, is it not? She carried him to his study and deposited him in a chair by the fire. She kissed me then, and I could taste his blood lingering upon her tongue.

"I must leave here," she said. "It will not be safe for me with him alive, fool though he is. Come with me."

I wanted to go. The enormity of life without her—I scarce could imagine going back to my dull, passionless existence. But I could not abandon a husband of fourteen years so abruptly. And there was Jeröen to consider. Twelve years old, he was. How could I leave before I saw him grow to manhood? "I cannot."

Her eyes flashed red again. Hurt, as much as anger, I think. But she did not try to persuade me further. "When he wakes," she said, "ask your so saintly husband what special ingredient laces those chocolates he brings you so regularly."

"What do you mean?"

"Ask him."

No final embrace. She passed out of my life as swiftly as she had entered.

Van was rousing, so I put aside my grief, placed my hand over his broad one, with its dusting of freckles and hair like fine copper wires. For the first time, I noticed the strands of gray in his reddish hair, the lines deepening about his eyes. So vulnerable he looked, and I felt a terrible fondness for him.

He pulled his hand from mine. His shoulders shook with the violence of his weeping.

Never had I seen a man so broken. I had done this to him, with my hedonist ways. So Adam must have wept when Eve gave him the forbidden fruit. Oh, but I was a weak, vile, creature.

Yet I pretended sternness. "Van," I said, "it is not the end of the world."

"It is the end of my world." He fumbled for his handkerchief. "How could you submit to the embrace of that—that—creature?" He looked at me with sudden, pitiable hope. "She coerced you, did she not? You were powerless against her. She is not human. She—"

"I love her." Better perhaps if I had lied, gave him a sop to his pride, but I could not. "The chocolates, Van," I said, "what is their special ingredient?"

He blinked through his tears. "Chocolates?"

"Yes, the ones you so kindly bring me every week. They are different from other confections, yes? I'd like to know how."

A simple question, to focus his scattered wits, but why did he look so startled, so guilty? Had he not felt so undone, I'm sure he would never have told me the truth. "Mercury," he said.

"Mercury?" I knew enough of his work to know mercury came from cinnabar, and that it was commonly used for disorders of the skin, and for centuries had been the preferred treatment for—for—

Though never prone to megrims, vapors, or any other form of weakness commonly experienced by my sex, I confess I sat down rather abruptly.

Mercury was the preferred treatment for pox.

I should not know such things, but Van had never denied me his books, and I read voraciously on matters medical as well as insectile. Pox. Morbus Gallicus. The French Disease. Or, if you were in France, the English Complaint. Also blamed upon the Spanish, Italians, Germans, and the New World.

Syphilis.

Dear God.

If I were tainted—would not my son be also, the disease carried through my milk to his innocent lips? The blood left my face. "Jeröen."

"Jeröen is healthy."

I closed my eyes. "Thank God."

"Yes. Thank God."

I might have railed, screamed, wept, but to what avail? I allowed Reason to reassert itself. Quite calmly I said, "So you have been visiting whores while I thought you were working?"

He turned red to the roots of his hair. "I have not," he said, mustering indignation from the depths of his shock and grief.

"Then you knew you were ill when you married me?" This seemed the greater crime, and my voice trembled with the enormity of it, in spite of my resolve.

He reached out his hand to me, thought better of it. "No. You must not think that. I would never—Marieke, I was ill, yes, but I knew not the cause. The disease mimics many other lesser illnesses. Symptoms can remain hidden for years, decades. When I knew the truth, it was too late."

"You might have told me."

"It is not a subject one speaks of to one's wife."

I pitied him, for the burden he had carried so long alone. He was as much a prisoner of circumstance as I. Yet his deception was years in duration and has killed me. Has killed us both. Not so swiftly as a knife, but with all the tenderness of the conjugal bed.

IV

Jeröen came home from school on spring holiday. Van Helsing loved his son, a round-faced, laughter-filled child of twelve. He had inherited his mother's fine intellect, but none of her seriousness. Indeed, Van Helsing frequently wondered where this happy stranger had come from. He had a generous, affectionate nature totally at odds with Marieke's cool reserve and his father's own awkward amiability.

"Papa!" Jeröen burst into the study without knocking.

The boy, three inches taller than when last Van Helsing had seen him, gave him a tight hug and kiss on both cheeks. Van Helsing returned the embrace firmly, then put both hands upon the boy's shoulders and studied him as intently as he would study a book. Too thin, Van Helsing thought. The boy was growing too fast. Indeed, he needed new clothes, for bony wrists jutted from his sleeves. One cuff bore a splatter of ink. "How is school?" Van Helsing asked.

"I'm doing well in Latin," Jeröen said, rearranging the items on the desk restlessly. "But Papa, don't you think Julius Caesar was a pompous bore? I told my professor I thought so, and he went all purple. I thought he would have an apoplexy right there and then. I told him he must come to Amsterdam and see you, since you are the finest doctor in all the city, the finest doctor in all the Low Countries."

Van Helsing laughed. He could not remember the last time he had felt like laughing. He ruffled Jeröen's blond hair. "How many guilders do you think to cozen out of me for that piece of flattery?"

Jeröen looked puzzled. "Not flattery, Papa. It's true. Everyone says so. Do you mind if I don't become a doctor, Papa? I'll never be as good as you, and to see people suffer—it quite makes me want to weep."

"A doctor's duty is to lessen suffering," Van Helsing said. "Still, you needn't study medicine. There's always law."

Jeröen's face fell. Van Helsing laughed again.

Compared to law, *Caesar's Commentaries* must seem the height of drama. Van Helsing squeezed his son's shoulder. "Relax, my boy. You need not choose a suitable career this very instant. Go greet your mother and let me return to my work."

"But I have chosen a career, Papa. I should like to be an actor. We saw a production of *Hamlet* last month. It was terribly exciting."

Van Helsing concealed a smile. No father would permit his son to choose so disreputable a career, but within the month or week, he knew Jeröen would light on some other passion, as Marieke's butterflies flitted from blossom to blossom. Art might be next, or astronomy, or soldiering. "*Hamlet*, eh?" he said. "And the sufferings of the wretches in that sad play did not make you weep?"

"Oh, I wept bitterly at the end. But it was only pretend. Will you come and see me in a play when I am an actor?"

"I should be honored," Van Helsing said. "Now, go say hello to your mother. I think she's in the garden."

"One more question, Papa?"

"Just one?"

"How do you know when you are in love?" Jeröen's fair face had flushed a deep red, but his eyes, blue, wide-set, earnest, held a rare seriousness.

Van Helsing felt his own face stiffen into a blankly pleasant mask. "We can talk about that later," he said.

Jeröen quit the study with a quick grin. His son, Van Helsing reflected, had the effect of the sun bursting through a pall of clouds. And when the great orb disappeared into cloud again, all seemed darker and colder than before. "Love," Van Helsing said softly to himself.

Jeröen found me in my garden, trying to recapture the pleasures I had once known with my studies of Lepidoptera. My thoughts turned ever toward Caterina. I should have gone with her when she asked. Jeröen was old enough to get by without me. Van would always have his work.

Jeröen sought out his father, first. He always did. This pained me now when it never had before. Had I not toiled in agony for hours to bring Jeröen into this world? And he goes first to the Great Deceiver?

"Papa says I may become an actor," he said, kissing my cheek.

I was sure Van had said nothing of the sort. "We are all of us actors," I said. "Only the stage is lacking." I tapped his wrist, frowning. "You've stained your cuff."

"Yes, Mama. I'm sorry. I was careless."

He shifted from foot to foot. The boy could never keep from fidgeting, no matter how much he tried. I always forgot how exhausting he could be. "Be still," I said, more sharply than I intended. "You will startle the butterflies."

He tried. But soon his fingers plucked at his jacket or drummed against my chair. "Why do you kill them?" he asked. "Aren't they prettier out here in the sun?"

"You sound like your father."

"Is he well? Papa seemed—I don't know—sad, somehow."

I admit to a total, irrational feeling of rage at this. Jeröen had no concern for my sadness. Weeks ago, I had a woman I loved, and a husband I respected. Now I lacked both. Van and I existed in cold silence, each outcast from the other's affection and trust.

The bees droned, sucking nectar from the trailing vines of wisteria and honeysuckle. They did not worry me. I'd always found that if you remained still and did not annoy them, the bees would reciprocate.

"Mama?"

One bee buzzed close by, and Jeröen batted at it nervously.

"Will you not be still?" I shouted.

The bee darted at Jeröen, stung him where pale throat met starched collar. Jeröen slapped at his neck, frantic, and gave a howl of pain. Uncharitably, I wished my son were made of sterner stuff. I did not realize the seriousness of the matter.

Jeröen collapsed, still clawing at his throat. The sting had made a great welt, and his face was swelling horribly. He gasped, seemed unable to catch his breath. I screamed to the servants to send my husband to me at once, knelt to loosen Jeröen's collar. I scraped the stinger away with my fingernail, held my boy's head upon my lap. His eyes were wide and terrified. "Shhh," I told him, brushing the hair back from his brow. "Your father is coming."

Van arrived quickly. The color left his face as he saw Jeröen's state. He swept the boy into his arms and carried him to his study. I hurried after.

He lay Jeröen upon the settee, took his pulse. Jeröen fought for every breath. His skin grew clammy beneath my anxious fingers. "Do something," I said. Why was the oh so famous Doctor Van Helsing dithering while his son lay dying? The great hands trembled. The brilliant eyes held uncertainty and panic. He did not know what to do.

Months have passed, and I believe now there is nothing he could have done. God took our boy to punish us both. But I hated my husband then, a hate that solidified with every tortured gasp Jeröen took.

Those gasps ceased. Five minutes only had lapsed between the sting and my son's death. Some form of shock, it was. A rare intolerance to the bee's venom. And I saw in Van's eyes that he blamed me as much as I blamed him. My garden, my insects, after all.

Van grieved as much as I. He threw himself into his work, closeted himself in his study. We had become living ghosts and neither of us sought to comfort the other.

I thought Caterina would return and take me away from this hell of grief and guilt, but she did not. So, I brooded, and imagined the syphilis biting into my bones, my heart, my brain, like a caterpillar devouring a cabbage leaf. The flesh fell from my bones like water. My eyes hated the light. My hands, claws now, trembled with weakness. My handwriting, once fine, firm, became nearly illegible.

When Van finally noticed how spectral I had become, he ordered me forcibly fed. The servants bound me, and ran a tube down my throat, poured broth into me through a funnel. I struggled and gagged and wept, but the disgusting violation was repeated daily. I grew convinced that Van meant to poison me in this fashion. After all, how far a stretch is it from mercury in sweets to arsenic in broth? Of course, I realize now that if he really wanted to murder me, he need have done nothing but leave me to my slow starvation.

V

1870

A damp, drizzly day. A busy day, weather notwithstanding. Van Helsing had spent the morning seeing patients at the almshouse, the afternoon performing a dissection for the medical students, revealing for their edification advanced disease of the aorta, undoubtedly the result of tertiary syphilis. He had a touch of catarrh, which the weather did not improve. The lecture left him hoarse.

He could have hired a cab to take him home from the operating theater, but the gloom suited him and he decided to walk. He moved slowly, for rain made the cobblestones slippery. He bowed his head against the cold drizzle and against a grief that continued undiminished since Jeröen's death a year ago this day.

The boy would have been thirteen now. At least Jeröen had gone to God an innocent, uncorrupted by carnality.

A bee sting. God, the irony. That such a small, beneficent creature, pollinator of flowers, maker of healthful honey and beeswax, a creature whose very name had become synonymous with useful industry, that such an insect should be the instrument of death to his only son—it was almost too much to be borne. And he, Van Helsing, physician of some note, though not as renowned as Jeröen had believed, had been as helpless as any other father to ease the swelling of the tortured throat, the wheezing of the labored lungs.

Nor could he forget Marieke's expression, no matter how much he tried. Without words she seemed to say, "Well, I knew you were not much of a man, but I thought you were at least a great doctor. Now I know you are neither."

Van Helsing lifted the latch of the iron gate, stepped into the cemetery. The grass squelched beneath his feet. He had no difficulty finding the grave. He visited often.

He traced his fingers over the carved letters, the cold of the stone penetrating deep in spite of his gloves. Jeröen Ambrosius Van Helsing, 1857-1869, Beloved Son.

Van Helsing took off his hat, the excess water cascading from the brim. "Hello, Jeröen," he said. "Your mother would visit if she could. She—she—" He drew a ragged breath, fighting tears. He plucked a handkerchief from within his coat. He coughed into the square of fabric, studied the mucus with a critical eye, wiped his nose, wadded the handkerchief and stuffed it into his pocket. Water dripped inside his collar. He shivered. "She is getting better." That was not quite a lie. She had seemed better. Pliant blankness was an improvement over naked hate, was it not? And they took very good care of her at the asylum.

"I've been invited to London. To teach at the Royal Academy of Surgeons. A great honor, but I've not yet accepted. I—I don't like the thought of leaving Amsterdam, leaving you, leaving your mother.

"I never answered your question that last day, did I? I thought we would have so much time, you see. I'm sorry. How do you know when you love someone? For me, it came like a sickness. When I would be near your mother, I felt as though dozens of her damned butterflies had flown into my stomach. I never knew if I was going to laugh or retch. And then one day the butterflies stopped. It hurts, my boy. It hurts so very much."

He put his sodden hat upon his head. "It grows late. We will talk again." Van Helsing turned away, tears blinding him as much as the worsening rain. He felt a sensation in his right hand, as if someone had placed a hand in his and squeezed it once. Ah, he was tired and unwell. The mind played tricks.

He arrived home thoroughly soaked and chilled. He took no supper, in spite of his housekeeper's remonstrance. The servants knew what day it was and had grown accustomed to his eccentricities. He did accept a towel and dry dressing gown from his valet. In spite of the generous blaze of the fire, more jenever than was perhaps good for him, and an extra shawl draped about his shoulders as he bent over his desk, he could not seem to banish the chill. He stared at the notes for the monograph he was writing on the evolution of brain matter. He was in no mood for it tonight.

A pain had begun behind his eyes. His chest felt tight. His throat, uncomfortably raw all day, now felt constricted, inflamed.

He should just seek his bed. Rest was a better medicine than any tonic, bolus, or salve in his cabinet. His eye fell upon the letter from the Royal Academy. He should write, decline their kind offer. After all, what use could he be to them, he who could not even cure himself of the catarrh? He thrust the letter into the pocket of his dressing gown.

Van Helsing rose, fought a momentary dizziness, no doubt the result of too much jenever on an empty stomach. He banked the fire, turned down the lamps, all but one. This he carried into the tiny adjoining room that still served him for bedchamber.

He'd reduced the household to three servants. He had no need of so large a dwelling. For one man—it was extravagant. He should sell, move to more modest quarters near the hospital.
Or take that post in England. Fly from this house with its attendant memories and grief. Longingly, he fingered the letter in his pocket. Let England ease the weight of a mad wife, a dead child, the bitterness of all his failures.

Yet how could he leave the house where he and Marieke had been so happy, even if that happiness had proven illusion only? How could he abandon the walls that had witnessed the birth and death of his son?

For the rooms rang with Jeröen's absent footfalls, fragments of remembered chatter, echoes of laughter. The boy seemed as much a part of the house as brick, tile, or plaster.

Van Helsing put the lamp upon a narrow table, removed his spectacles, climbed beneath the cool, crisp sheets with a sigh.

A strange noise woke him just after midnight. He lay quite still, holding the wheeze of his breath a moment, the better to tell if the noise came again.

So slight a sound, he might have dreamed it. A sort of scrape or hollow knock. Van Helsing rose, fumbled for his spectacles.

His pillow was soaked with sweat, and his nightclothes clung damply to him. He shivered as the night air, so great a contrast from his overheated bed, plucked at him. The smell of his sweat reminded him of fried potatoes. He was thirsty, but his throat felt so hot and painful, he did not think he would be able to swallow. Indeed, his own spittle conspired to choke him.

A warm saltwater gargle would help, perhaps. Once he had investigated the mysterious sound. He lit the wick of the lamp, turned the flame high in spite of the stabbing pain the brightness brought his eyes. He placed the globe back over the wick, lifted the lamp, and crossed to his study.

A thud of something falling to the rug, and a softer sound, a wordless rhythmic whispering, unlike anything he had ever heard before. Hallucination, he thought. A product of fever.

For no one was in the room. All looked mostly as he had left it. Oh, the framed purple emperor butterfly Marieke had given him as a wedding gift had tumbled inexplicably from the corner of his desk, but that was all.

He stooped, curled his fingers around the dark wooden frame, the cool oval of convex glass. He was dismayed to note the glass had cracked. The specimen itself remained undamaged, very secure upon its pin.

The wings moved.

Van Helsing nearly dropped the frame in startlement. Wings fluttered slowly and then with increased agitation, brushing against the glass. Whispering.

Impossible.

The thing was dead. Had been dead for at least fifteen years, for this was the same *apatura iris* Marieke had been mounting the day he proposed to her. Dead things did not live again.

Seizing a letter opener from his desk drawer, he pried the back from the frame, lifted off the ruined glass. The wings fluttered even more madly now. Van Helsing seized the pin, pulled it free of the board, free of the thorax of the impossibly reanimated butterfly. The purple emperor lifted in flight, circled the glow of the lamp, disappeared into the shadows of dark beams overhead.

Van Helsing seized the lamp, opened the door of his study, climbed the narrow, curving stairs, his hand damp upon the polished balustrade. More frames, more brightly painted wings in airless struggle. The frames, ornate as any housing a Rembrandt or Hals, banged against floral wallpaper, tilted on their hooks.

Wings. Small, large, bright, dull, European native or tropical exotic shipped from Brazil, Sumatra, the Congo. Azure, green, gold, spotted, streaked, splotched, delicately veined swallowtail, muddy-colored wood nymph. Wings battered against glass and screamed. Screamed.

Van Helsing broke the glass, plucked the pins away, felt blood ooze in sticky red from his fingers, but did not care. He barely registered the glass slicing into fingertips, palms, the backs of his hands. He grasped each pin, pulled it free. Wings lifted, fluttered about him, lit upon his nightshirt, his hair, walked upon exposed skin with a strange, light suction, like a hundred kisses.

He raced up the stairs in the dark, lamp forgotten. He knew the way, knew he must free them all, the thousands of souls Marieke had collected for so long. He smashed the cases in her study. A cloud of butterflies surrounded him. Wings cooled his fevered flesh, whispered, whispered.

He spun about the room, heedless of the glass beneath his bare feet. Dark. Dark. He could not see. He fumbled for the window catch, swung the mullioned glass inward, threw open the wooden shutters. The rain had stopped. A cold moonlight spilled on him.

He danced with Marieke's butterflies, felt their soft caress against his swollen throat, his lips, his eyelids, the thinly fleshed bones of his ankles. He whirled with them, laughed in euphoric delight. He could fly with them. Fly.

Dizzy, fighting now for breath, he stumbled. Prisoned by his bulk once more, he sank to his knees. Alas, to remain earthbound, trapped in coarse clay. The butterflies streamed over him before winging away into the cool night. So many. Death had undone so many. More things in heaven and earth. Marieke would be angry.

He rolled onto his back, watched the butterflies flutter out the open window. A last one, the purple emperor, paused, flitted about his head, as it had earlier circled the lamp's light.

"Jeröen," Van Helsing said, his voice little more than a whisper from his sore throat.

Nonsense. The butterfly was older than Jeröen had been at death. Yet it pleased him to imagine his son's soul a tangible thing, and free; pleased him, too, that this one above all others seemed reluctant to leave him, kept hovering protectively, as if it forgave him all his follies.

"Go," he said. "You mustn't worry about me."

VI

It's a year now since Jeröen's death. I think. It is difficult to keep time in an asylum.

It's not so dreadful here, except they won't let me have any books. The learned doctors believe it was books drove me mad. The feminine mind should not be over-stimulated. Rubbish. I will ask Van to make them reconsider.

He visits me every Sunday after Church. After Mass, I should say. Van converted recently. The Church gives him comfort. He even wears a cross about his neck. The idolatry of it offends me. But Dutch Reformed or Papist, it matters not. I have no use for a God that will murder a child to punish the parent.

There is a certain liberation in madness. One can say what one thinks. I have even learned to swear.

But I have been good of late. Quiet. They believe I am vastly improved.

Not that they would say so to me. Learned men do not converse with madwomen. Learned men do not converse with women, mad or not. At least Van was different in that regard.

On his last visit, he told me my butterflies were gone. He said he wanted to prepare me, so I would not be unduly upset when I came home. It was the first time he had spoken of my coming home.

"Gone?" I asked.

"I set them free." He spoke very softly and took my hand. Scabs marred his palms and the backs of his hands, felt rough upon my skin. How they must have bled.

"It was wrong to imprison them," he said. "You do see that?"

I frowned, puzzled. "Are you talking about the butterflies in the garden?"

"No, Marieke. The ones upon the wall. They've all flown away."

"Husband," I said, "those butterflies are dead. The dead do not fly." How is it, I wondered, that I am in an asylum and my husband is not?

"It was a miracle," he said. "I think perhaps Jeröen's spirit had something to do with it."

I pulled my hand away. The syphilis had begun to eat his brain, I decided. It hurt to hear my son's name upon his lips.

I remembered Caterina's final kiss, remembered the taste of blood. I imagined Van's blood flowing into my mouth, filling me, all heat and salt and copper. The thought made me smile.

Van smiled back and I had to suppress a laugh. Poor fool.

"I will not be able to visit you for a little while, but I will write you from London." He kissed me, very sweetly, upon my brow.

I knew what I must do. I had been foolish to think Caterina would return for me. I must prove myself worthy, free myself from my prison. I will drink the blood of evil men.

Van I will spare, for Jeröen's memory, for remembrance of love. In spite of his deception, his disease, his ineptitude, his chocolates, he is a kindly man. But there are others. Like the new orderly who forces himself upon the charity cases. He is a brute. I will have no difficulty seducing him. He will not live long enough to know the gnawing of the syphilitic caterpillar. I will take his seed into my womb, and his blood into my mouth. My skin will run with blue flame. I will burst from the constricting chrysalis of this despised female form a fearsome avenger. I will glut myself on the red nectar. True, I have not Caterina's fangs, not yet. After I drink, perhaps. Or after I die. And then they will fear me.

Poison in the Darkness originally appeared in the 2004 anthology *The Many Faces of Van Helsing*, edited by Jeanne Cavelos.

Rita Oakes writes horror, dark fantasy, and historical fiction. A graduate of the Odyssey Writing Workshop, she enjoys history, travel, and Belgian beer-- sometimes at the same time. Her work has been published in the anthologies *The Many Faces of Van Helsing, Time Well Bent,* and *Zombies: Shambling through the Ages*. Most recently, her stories appeared in *Cosmic Horror Monthly, Dracula Beyond Stoker (One Bite), Beneath Ceaseless Skies*, and *New Myths*. In addition, she has a story collection, *Comrades-in-Arms,* from Lethe Press.

The Darkest Obsession
By Maxwell I. Gold

Inked in blood and adorned in letters too ancient to recount; I watched the fall of an evil so unspeakable I couldn't stop until there was nothing left. Not a single grain of sand, nor ash, or metal, dared remain while I walked this earth under blood stained spires that scratched the skies; except an obsession that tore me apart from the inside.

Ripped wide like some unimaginable schism cleaved from the bones of gods, bones, there before me, my soul soon ruptured and boiled over with the darkest phantoms chasing me through castle fog and unholy nights. This dark obsession, so uncontrollable and maddening sought my own destruction even when I defanged the monster; that which was most unbelievable, my dark fixation, and wretched seemed more pleasurable than this.

Maxwell I. Gold is a Jewish-American author and poet with an extensive body of work comprising over 350 poems and nine poetry collections since 2017. His work has appeared in numerous literary journals, magazines, and anthologies. Maxwell's work has earned nominations for two Bram Stoker Awards as well as the Eric Hoffer Award, Pushcart Prize, and Rhysling Award. Find him and his work at www.thewellsoftheweird.com.